I0761054

A SLEUTH IS BORN

A BETTY SNICKERDOODLE MYSTERY (#2)

PEPPER FROST

WORKING STRATEGY

THIS IS A WORK OF FICTION. Names, characters, businesses, places, events, locales, and incidents are either the products of the author's imagination or used in a fictitious manner. Any resemblance to actual persons, living or dead, or actual events is purely coincidental.

ISBN-13: 978-1-970044-11-9 [Paperback, large print]

To contact the author, please visit pepperfrostauthor.com. Or email her at pepper@pepperfrostauthor.com

To learn first about new releases and special offers, sign up for Pepper's newsletter at her website.

Pepper's on Facebook, too, at facebook.com/pepperfrostauthor

.

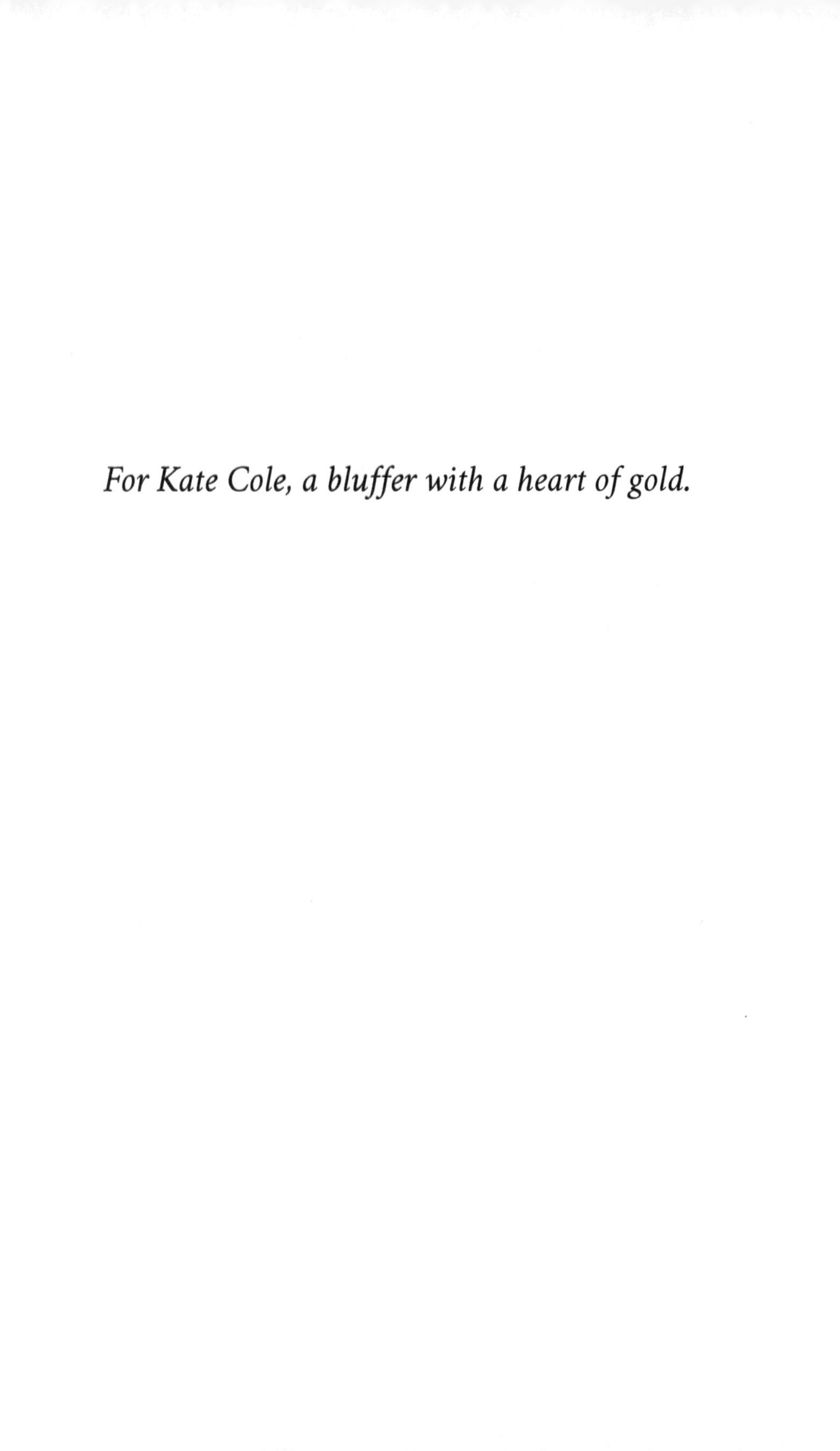

For Kate Cole, a bluffer with a heart of gold.

CHAPTER 1

In scruffy slippers and a threadbare nightie nearly as old as she was, Bea Sickles stared through the sunlit picture windows of her cozy suite. The view outside Betty Snickerdoodle's Christmas Inn & Ranch—the inn she owned and now called home—was undeniably breathtaking.

Thanks to late-fall rains, Napa Valley was blanketed in bright emerald green. Cheerful Christmas decorations had been lovingly tacked to practically every nearby structure. Wisps of fog floated above the miles of picturesque, rolling vineyards that surrounded the inn's grounds, and snow caps dotted the mountains that bordered the valley.

What a precious wine country Christmas scene,

thought Bea. *Just sprinkle in a few magical falling snowflakes and you can crank my crabby right up to 11*! She reached above her messy helmet of thin gray hair and snapped the drapes shut with a force that belied her age and tiny size.

Her current mood aside, Bea had no gripe with Christmas. How could she? Christmas had been very, very good to her. Over more than 20 years, she'd written dozens of bestselling Christmas romance novels under her Betty Snickerdoodle pen name. Her sweet holiday stories had made her a wealthy woman. Not bad for a second career, especially one started at an age when most people are longing to retire.

In fact, the wild success of those books enabled her to buy the inn and—with the help of her brilliant young business partner, Angela Garcia—pursue her vision of a Christmas-themed destination for Betty's fans.

But despite her gift for writing about them, Bea was not much like her Christmas-spirit-filled characters. She relied on her prolific imagination to build the world of Treacle Town and invent all the little dramas its inhabitants experienced. Her creativity and flair for sweet tales of love and the holidays had never once failed her—until now.

"My muse is on snooze!" Bea whined aloud.

She was experiencing her first bout of writer's block, and the timing couldn't have been worse.

The inaugural BettyCon convention, planned to coincide with the inn's grand opening, was just a few weeks away. More than 100 Betty Snickerdoodle superfans would flock to the inn to celebrate their love of Betty Snickerdoodle and Treacle Town. To help make the occasion even more special, Bea had told Angela she'd write a brand-new Betty story. The ardent fans at BettyCon would be thrilled to be the first to read it.

She'd assumed that dreaming up a new tale would be a piece of cake—just like always. Who knew a blank page could be an instrument of torture?

Inspiration should have been easy to find. Every decoration in her suite, like all the rooms in the inn, was drawn from Betty's world—from the murals inspired by vintage wrapping paper, to the red-ribboned wreath above the suite's fireplace, to the gingerbread candles that gave the bathroom its glorious scent of spiced molasses.

Bea was practically soaking in the spirit of Christmas. Still, the ideas just weren't coming.

Bea sighed and shuffled back to her computer to try again. But her gaze was drawn away from the screen to the perfect little Christmas tree on the back corner of her desk. Someone had placed it there so thoughtfully. Someone had decorated it with such care! She stretched her crooked fingers toward the jingle-bell ornament dangling from one of the branches—an exquisitely scaled-down bauble that tinkled sweetly as the desk moved. Then she flicked it, sending it sailing into the air. It crashed onto the hardwood with a defiantly cheerful jingle. Somehow, it didn't even break.

Be quiet, would ya? I'm trying to think.

It was rare for anything to upend Bea's steely self-confidence, but negativity had somehow taken the reins of her imagination. *What if my Betty-writing days are behind me?* she wondered morosely, until the sound of a bell interrupted her budding pity party. She looked down at the silent, motionless ornament on the floor with scorn—then let out a hearty cackle when she realized the sound had come from her laptop.

A message on the screen said, "Betty Snicker-doodle has seventeen new book reviews."

Hmm. Didn't Angela always say fans have great ideas for Treacle Town? Let's see what Betty's loyal supporters have to say!

Bea clicked on the sales page for *Treacle Town ♥ Christmas,* Betty's newest release. She and Angela had decided to offer it for free, as a gift to fans.

What on earth? The page was filled with new reviews all right—terrible ones. Every one of them emblazoned with a symbol Bea had never even seen before: the dreaded one-star rating.

"I think this might be fake literature. What ever that is. Loser literature. Just don't," read one.

Said another: "I dont like Betty and I dont like Christmas. There r already 2 many books about that stupid holiday!!"

"The book is bad. Dumb people falling in love at Christmas and getting a second chance. Yes, I know thats all it claims to be. It should be more exciting. Betty is a loser."

"No book deserves so many five stars. I'm giving it one. Who died and made Betty Snickerdoodle the Queen of Christmas? Don't give Betty any more money. Yes I know its free. So what. Don't be a loser."

> *"I wish I could give it zero stars. I think it should be banned. Its terrible. And its way too short!!"*

THAT LAST ONE burned Bea up the most.

She interlocked her fingers and stretched her arms in front of her. After pantomiming a few flamboyant piano strokes to warm up her creaky joints, Bea clicked the "author reply" link.

Dear Birdbrain,

You complain that you don't like my book, yet it's also too short. Are you unhappy when it rains, and even unhappier when it stops? At restaurants, do you gripe about receiving too little of a food you dislike?
Have you ever wished for a longer vacation—in prison?
My books are not written for dodos like you.
As for banning, you might be onto something.
Why don't you go ban yourself?

Most sincerely,
Betty Snickerdoodle

Bea reread her work, pleased. But as she was about to click "post," a pesky memory popped into her head.

"Bea," she heard Angela saying, "If we get a negative review, promise me you won't reply. It's OK to say thank you for positive ones. But we don't engage with negative ones."

"If you say so," Bea recalled responding, not thinking much about it. Bea didn't care much, or know much, about social media. Plus, the stakes were low. Betty Snickerdoodle had never received anything but glowing reviews.

"But Angie, I'm curious. Why can't we reply?"

"It's a well-known best practice in social media marketing," Angela had declared. "You can't win if you engage with haters."

Being told she couldn't win or couldn't do something because of some rule summoned Bea's resistance faster than a can opener calls a cat. But she'd put Angela in charge of such matters, and she'd promised she wouldn't reply. So she wouldn't. She didn't have to be happy about it, though.

Grrr, she thought, scrolling back through the idiotic reviews. Angela couldn't have imagined reviews this stupid when she decreed that "no replying" would be company policy.

Bea backspaced through her reply, one letter at a time, scowling.

Click. Click. Click. Sigh.

Click. Click. Click. Sigh.

But as she deleted her snarky reply, she noticed something odd. The bad reviews all appeared under different handles, yet seemed… similar, somehow. She puzzled over it for a moment, furrowing her silvery brows.

"Eureka!" she exclaimed. For weeks, an idea had been germinating in her subconscious. Now, it seemed, was its time to sprout.

"Rebecca," she announced, awakening the tubular internet speaker in the corner. The lights on top of it signaled it had come to attention. "Call Pat Rogers."

"Calling Pat Rogers, private investigator," purred the tube's silky artificial voice.

Pat answered with a gruff hello.

"Pat, it's Bea Sickles—you know, Betty Snickerdoodle. I've got a problem and you can help. It's my Christmas-story mojo—I seem to have lost it."

"My job involves finding lost things, Bea… but I wouldn't know where to begin to find a lost mojo," Pat said. She was trying to sound nonchalant to disguise her surprise. The only time they'd met, she'd accused Bea of burglary and stranded her in San Francisco. The incident hadn't left Pat with the impression she'd made a friend.

"Ha! Good one, girl," cackled Bea. "You've improved my mood already. So here's my idea. My Christmas muse is on the lam, maybe for good. I need a new genre. I've been thinking about mysteries, like that Jessica Fletcher. But I don't know how to solve crimes. I need a fast tutorial on detecting—and you're just the gal to provide it."

"I'm flattered, but why am I just the gal?"

"Primarily because you're the only detective I know," Bea said. "Besides, Charlie trusts you." Pat had an office right next door to Bea's longtime agent and friend, Charlie Carter. In fact, it was Charlie's office Pat accused Bea of breaking into.

"Are you around over the holidays? If you come to the inn on the 21st and stay a few days, I'll pay you double your day rate. What say you?"

"Sounds like an offer I can't refuse."

"I've even got a little mystery for us to practice on. I'll tell you about it when you get here."

This whodunit thing will be a gas, Bea thought. She was looking forward to inventing some obnoxious characters and killing them off. In the sugar-crusted Christmas utopia of Treacle Town, everyone lived happily ever after *forever,* regardless of how annoying they were.

Nothing invigorated Bea like a plan. She decided to start by checking out her mystery novel competition. But first, a little exercise to get the blood flowing.

"Rebecca, play 'Watching the Detectives.' Louder!" She danced around her suite with her characteristic ungainly abandon. As the song ended, she flopped down on her bed, laughing.

The internet tube flashed to life again. Three soft boop-boop-boops came from its speaker.

"Angela calling," Rebecca announced.

"Bea, you decent?" asked Angela.

"No. I'm great. Surely you know that by now."

"You know what I mean. Are you dressed? I've got big news. How soon can you meet me in the ballroom?"

"I'll come right now if I can wear my nightie." Bea hopped down from her chair, checked out her pint-sized profile in the full-length mirror, and let loose a bark of laughter at her own appearance. The fabric of her cotton nightgown was so worn and thin, the floral print was barely visible. "On the plus side, it's my most opaque one."

"I can wait. How about you put on street clothes and I'll see you in 15 minutes? And don't forget proper undergarments."

"Sure thing, girlie."

Her news can't be as exciting as mine, thought Bea, pulling her brown stirrup pants up to meet the band of the bra she'd reluctantly put on. *But I must find the right moment to tell her, and the right way, too, or she'll get upset and worry that a new genre would be too big a gamble. For such a smart and ambitious young person, Angie is a real fraidy-cat sometimes.*

On top of a dingy mock turtleneck, Bea added a tasteful Christmas-themed cardigan—one of Angela's recent acquisitions for the gift shop. It had a classic Fair Isle snowflake design, with antique metal buttons on a deep carmine background.

"Sweet. Classy. Bo-ring," she said to the mirror, shaking her head. She shrugged. "Angie will love it."

She stepped into her sheepskin boots, smoothed her bob with a swipe of a brush, and grabbed her cane. As she slammed the suite's door behind her, the jingle bell decoration someone had hooked on the peephole chimed softly.

"Chime all you want, bell," cackled Bea. "Your Christmas spirit won't bring me down now!"

CHAPTER 2

"Please sit down, Bea," Angela said. She'd pulled a few of the chairs off a stack that sat on the side of the inn's large, mostly empty ballroom. She looked pretty as ever, but all business, too, her thick, brown hair in a bun held in place with a pencil. Her expression suggested she had big news to share. "I've got something to tell you. I think it will make you feel better."

"Better than what?" said Bea.

"You—you've seemed out of sorts lately. Have you been feeling bad about everyone leaving for the holidays?"

Bea had not confessed to Angela the trouble she'd had writing the new book she'd promised—and she wasn't about to cop to it now.

"Angie, how come you don't know by now I don't have feelings? It's deeply disappointing."

"Disappointment is a feeling."

"It's just a logical reaction to my reasonable expectations not being met."

"Prickliness is also a feeling. Shall I tell you my news?"

"Prickliness is a trait, not a feeling. You're confused about feelings, Angie. But don't worry, I still love you."

"Love is a feeling!" Angela laughed.

"You know that's not how I meant it. I'm responding appropriately to all you've done to make Betty a big success. And to all the fun we have together."

"Desperation to win an argument is a feeling. And it's irrational."

"Low blow." To Bea, "irrational" might be the ultimate insult—particularly when delivered along with superior logic.

"OK," Bea sighed. "Let's hear the big idea. No, wait, let me guess: Bea, it's the perfect time to write a new Betty book! It'll be great to have for BettyCon! Bea, you'll have the entire inn to yourself! It will be so quiet! Blah blah blah. I heard you the first ten times."

"I'd love to have that new Betty book, but that's not what I was planning to tell you."

"Good, because I've got a new plan for our quiet time, and I'm looking forward to it."

"That's too bad, because it looks like we'll have less quiet time. I've booked us a nice piece of business. I think you're going to be excited about it," Angela said, beaming.

"Go on."

"It's a private three-day poker tournament for multimillionaires—an exclusive, high-stakes getaway. The client thought that since we're not open yet, we'd keep her event low-profile. Protecting her millionaires' privacy is her big concern. No one knows about the event—it's a super-exclusive, invitation-only thing."

Bea's eyebrows ascended to the fringe of her bangs. Angela squared her shoulders, sat up a little straighter, and forged on.

"I don't have to tell you there'll be lots of cash on hand for the poker. Thousands of dollars—that's another reason we have to keep it low-profile. Oh, and it's for charity. Isn't it exciting? It will be like a practice run for our official opening next month. I call it our Christmas bluebird—a fantastic piece of business that dropped right into our laps."

"Might be a special gift from Santa," Bea said. "More likely, we're getting a scam in our stocking."

"What?" Angela grumbled.

"Angie, who plans a big, secret charity event with only a few days' notice—right before Christmas? Especially an event for high-rollers."

"Well, Bea, maybe you should let me finish. She didn't just start planning it. She said she's been doing it for years. But her regular venue—a lodge up in Paradise—burned down in that wildfire. She figured she'd have to cancel at this late date, but, luckily, she heard about our inn."

"Oh, Paradise. Those poor folks. What a sweet little Gold Rush town. And those big trees! It was my cheap getaway when I first started writing as Betty. More like free, since I usually picked up a few bucks at the Indian casinos nearby," she chuckled. In the years before she became a writer, Bea had scratched out a modest living as a small-stakes poker player. "But Angie, this has to be a scam. You haven't seen as many scams as I have. Trust me."

"How about you trust *me* a little, Bea? I didn't just fall off the turnip truck, you know. I have already received a 50% deposit," Angela said, sighing and crossing her arms. "That's a fact, not a feeling.

Cold, hard, factual cash is already in my hot little hand."

"OK, let's say it's not a scam. Aren't you worried about putting this thing together so fast? The staff's mostly gone for Christmas already. And I know how you love work, Angie, but don't you have any plans of your own for the holidays?"

"She's offered $50,000. We can afford to pay overtime. She says the players are big tippers, too. Two servers and two housekeepers have signed up already. Plus, we're only providing continental breakfast—the chef will make dinners and a few snacks, but the hostess is even providing ingredients. If we pull it off, there'll be a lot more to celebrate on Christmas. We'll have a profitable year before we even open!"

"She offered $50,000? For some muffins and a few room nights? Yeah, that sure sounds like it's on the up-and-up," Bea snorted.

"We've already got our $25,000 deposit. Even if she skips out on the balance, we easily break even. Plus, if we pull this off, we might become *the* place for exclusive VIP retreats. The potential is amazing!" Visions of posh events galore were already dancing in Angela's ambitious imagination.

Bea was about to remind Angela that the inn was intended to be a place for Betty's fans—not a playpen for the upper crust. But another set of gears was turning in her head. Millionaires, high-stakes poker, a sneaky scam of some sort—it was all sounding like inspiration for the wine country's answer to Agatha Christie.

"I guess if the $25,000 covers our costs, we can risk it. You should decide, Angie. You're the president, right? I think you should go on and tell me about the poker part."

"Hooray!" Angela said, pleased to win the argument, even if not sure how she did it. "What I know so far is they'll play three tournaments over three nights: the 21st, 22nd, and 23rd. Each tournament has an equal winner-take-all prize pool, about $100,000 after our fee and the charity's. Players each buy in for all three—$45,000 for the prize pool and a $5,000 donation to the charity."

"$45,000 buy-in? Holy guacamole!"

"$50,000 altogether—the donation is mandatory. Would you like to play? They've got nine players and room for one more."

Angela knew that Bea had never played stakes like that. She could easily afford $50K now, though. Bea had banked millions from her Betty Snickerdoodle novels and spent almost none of it, living like a hermit in a modest little cottage for years. Besides, Angela figured, if Bea played, she'd probably win at least one of the three games and come out way ahead.

"Maybe I should play. Someone needs to keep an eye on all that money. You're talking about a half-million bucks sloshing around here. Will Mr. Tall Dark and Handsome be around to help? He could stand guard at the door in a tux, like a James Bond movie—provided you won't go all weak in the knees," Bea said. "I bet those millionaires expect a fancy-schmancy atmosphere."

Angela rolled her eyes. "You mean Aseem, I assume? Yes, I asked him to help get the place ready and add some security."

Bea's innuendo annoyed Angela—mainly because it was 100% correct. Her knees were already a little wobbly at the thought of Aseem in a tux. But she knew Aseem had always seen her as just his friend—and now also as his boss.

"Could you try to be professional for a minute? I need your help with the poker—tables, dealers, all that stuff."

"Yes, Madam President!" said Bea. She hopped down from her chair and gave Angela a mock salute. "I'll work on it. I'll see if Perry can help."

Perry was the boss at a local card room and an old pal of Bea's from her poker days. They went back decades. Angela suspected they'd been more than friends, but Bea was tight-lipped on the subject.

"If he can't help, he'll know someone who can. By the way, do we have enough rooms done, Angie?"

"We'll need 10 all together for the nine players and the organizer. Should fill up the rooms we've finished renovating."

"Sounds like we might be short a few. Won't we need rooms for Perry and Aseem? Plus I invited Pat Rogers to come for a visit." Bea decided this was not the time to reveal she planned to put her holiday romance novels on pause to try her hand at mysteries. Better to be vague about her reasons for inviting Pat. "I invited her a few days ago—when I thought I'd be all alone here."

"Pat Rogers? The pushy PI who falsely accused you of breaking into Charlie's office?"

"Yeah, yeah, but she didn't mean anything by it. Besides, I kind of like her. She's a tough broad. She reminds me of the fun we had crushing Cash." Cash was a bumbling criminal who'd tried to get rich quick by stealing a manuscript from Bea months before, foolishly believing he was taking advantage of a meek, defenseless little old lady. Bea had loved serving Cash his just deserts (with Angela's clever assistance). Cash had been arrested and charged and would soon be relocated to new digs, courtesy of the Department of Corrections. With any luck, he'd be their guest for the remainder of his 20s.

"Bea, as I remember it, Pat almost gave Cash the upper hand. Plus, she stranded you in San Francisco without a ride back to Napa." The incident was not something Angela would soon forget. The truth was, she'd been partly responsible for Bea being stranded in the city. The episode turned out to be a grand adventure for Bea, but that didn't stop Angela from feeling guilty about it.

"But where are your manners, Angie? It's too late for me to uninvite her, I'm sure you agree. Bygones?"

"I guess if you forgive her, I can, too. But that means we're definitely short a room."

"Maybe Aseem will just have to sleep with you," Bea cackled, slapping her knee.

Angela's face turned pink and grumpy. "Boundaries, Bea?"

Eventually, Bea stopped cackling at her own joke. "OK, OK. What about one of the new casitas the crew's been working on? We could put someone there. Not the charity lady, though—I think we should keep a close eye on her."

"There's one almost completed. It's not quite finished enough for a guest, but Aseem could stay there," Angela agreed.

"Speaking of the charity lady, what do we know about her? Who's wrangling these poker-playing millionaires?"

"Her name's Lee Glastonbury. She didn't say much about herself. I haven't found much about her or her charity online, either. I guess we'll learn more when she gets here."

With rare restraint, Bea bit her lip and suppressed the urge to blurt out "scam" again.

"Have I got my marching orders? I'll go call Perry right now."

"One more thing. You were right about fancy-schmancy. The evening events are black tie optional. We get to dress up! Isn't that fun?"

"Oh goody," groaned Bea. "I'll figure out something."

CHAPTER 3

"Well if it isn't my old gal Bea. Or should I call you Mabel? Or is it Betty?" Perry was possibly the one person on Earth who knew all of Bea's poker and pen names.

"You can call me whatever you want. But how come you never call me?"

"Phone works in both directions, dearest Bea. To what do I owe the honor of your call?"

"We've booked a three-night private tournament for multimillionaires at the inn—starting the night of December 21st, before we even open. You up for a last-minute tournament director gig?"

"They're just planning it now?"

"That's not even the strangest part. It's supposed to be for charity—real high-rollers. So the buy-in's $50,000..."

"You've got my attention."

"... and each night is a single-table tourney with a winner-take-all cash prize. $100,000+."

"Holy cow."

"Ever heard of a tournament like this?"

"No."

"Sound legit?"

"Hell no."

"That's what I thought."

"It sounds like a scam," Perry laughed. "But it sure sounds like fun."

"I was hoping you'd say so," Bea said. "I figure we'll need two tables—one will be for a side game. Plus two dealers and an ace tournament director—you, I hope. Short notice, but what do you think?"

"Have tables, will travel. We also got these fancy Christmas decks and tournament chips from our vendor as a gift. The Victorian designs aren't much of a match for our, uh, unpolished cardroom crowd. Could be perfect for your occasion. I've even got the perfect detail cop if you need security help. Nice guy, not weighed down by excessive diligence about the law. Is your alter ego Mabel going to play in these big games?"

"I think it should be my alter ego Betty, since her name's on the door of this little guest house. I want to keep an eye on all that money. Bring the fancy cards. This thing's all about fancy. And Perry, you're welcome to stay here, but you might have to share a room with one of the staff—we're running short."

"We could always bunk together, Bea. Like old times."

Bea groaned. "Tell me you're not going all nostalgic on me."

"Can I help it if some of my fondest memories are of you robbing my cradle all those years ago? For a romance writer, you're not very romantic."

"Truth is, the spirit willing, but the flesh is… not where it used to be," snickered Bea.

"I still see the old you."

"How do you know I'm not talking about you? But speaking of old you and old me, it'll be fun doing a poker thing together again."

"Indeed. Can I get a partial stake? I like your chances."

"We haven't even seen the competition yet."

"I always like your chances. Especially knowing those suckers will think they're playing sweet little old Betty Snickerdoodle."

"I've got a hunch this tourney won't be clean."

"Two sets of eyes on the action won't hurt."

"One other minor detail. You have to dress 'black tie optional,' whatever that means."

Perry chuckled. "I'll figure something out."

"Can't be a t-shirt with a tux painted on it. Think Casino Monte-Carlo."

"I'm more curious what you're going to come up with. You seem to forget I wear a jacket and tie in my day job. You, on the other hand—"

"That reminds me—"

"Yes, my dear?"

"I'm glad you'll be wearing a jacket, because I think you should bring that gun of yours. Just in case."

"Already on my list."

"Oh, and Perry, one more thing," Bea said. "It's not robbing the cradle when the younger person is doing the pursuing. If you're gonna get all goopy about ancient history, at least get it right."

"Tomayto, tomahto," said Perry with a laugh.

CHAPTER 4

Angela stood precariously on top of a stepladder, reaching high to tack a bushy garland above the fireplace mantel. She'd already attached one side and draped the evergreen strand underneath the huge wreath hanging above the fireplace. Now she wanted to tack the other end on the left side to create an elegant swoop effect, like a picture she'd seen in a high-society magazine.

She groaned softly as she stretched, standing a bit shakier on the tiptoes of her pristine white canvas sneakers. Just a smidge higher….

A bright, familiar voice entering the ballroom broke her concentration.

"Hey Angel!" Aseem said. He was heading toward her, holding up a ball of green foliage on a red satin ribbon. "Where would you like it?"

Angela turned her head slightly, focusing on maintaining her balance. But the sight of Aseem, now standing right next to her and dangling the leafy ball over his head of thick, wavy black hair, was a distraction.

"Is that—" she said as she began to teeter. But before she could say another word, she sensed herself falling. Thinking fast, Aseem reached out and deftly caught her in a classic threshold-carry position.

"What were you saying, Angel?" Aseem said, calmly placing her back on her feet.

"Thank you," Angela croaked. "That green ball —is it mistletoe?"

"Could be. Bea said you'd know what it was for."

Angela's face reddened and her eyes narrowed as she imagined Bea's cackling. Her knee was no doubt bruised from all the slapping.

"How about over there? Above the center patio door?"

"Perfect." Aseem carried the stepladder across the big room toward the three sets of custom French doors. More than a dozen feet high and topped by elegant transom windows, the doors led to a vast patio deck with sweeping views of the wine country. They were the capstone of the detailed renovation of the ballroom that Angela had completed just days before.

"Let me help you hang that decoration after I do this one, Angel. I don't want you falling off that ladder again. Don't you know you're not supposed to stand on the top step?" Angela wondered whether he was being chivalrous or commenting on her clumsiness.

"Perry should be here soon to set up the poker tables. He wanted to know if you've got the video recording set up—and the safe."

"Tech's good to go. See the camera up in the corner? Discreet, but visible enough to let everyone know they're on camera. It's motion-sensitive, too. Anyone who tries to tamper with it will end up being recorded."

"Perfect. Perry says it's mostly about deterrence, but it's good we'll also have evidence if we need it."

"The new safe's in the control room to the left of the stage. The computer server that will store the videos is tucked in there, too. It all fit perfectly —want to check it out?"

"No need, as long as it's Perry- and Bea-approved, it works for me. I'm so glad you know how to pull all this tech together so fast. Can the safe hold all that cash?"

"Yep. Turns out money doesn't take up much space at all. It would all fit in a shopping bag. Plenty of room for the chips, too."

"Bea's hoping you'll be standing guard at the door. She has this idea you'll be all dressed up in a tux, like Monte Carlo or something." She was stammering again. Damned visions of Aseem dressed up like a suave superspy.

"I wouldn't miss it—even if I have to rent a penguin suit. How often do you get to hang out with a bunch of multimillionaires throwing stacks of hundred-dollar bills around? Are you ready? I can help you get that garland tacked up now."

Angela was staring at the ginormous flat-screen monitor hanging on the wall at the back of the stage. The display would be impressive at their upcoming BettyCon fan event, but didn't really fit the vibe of their posh poker retreat. It would be hard enough to create a cozy and exclusive ambience in such a large room without the party being dwarfed by such a large piece of technology.

"Don't suppose we can take that screen down, can we?"

"I doubt it. It took six guys to install it originally."

Angela sighed. “It’s not very elegant. Can we decorate it to make it fit in better?”

“Sure,” said Aseem. “Let me try.” Aseem picked several garlands from the box on the floor and looped them around the rim of the monitor. He paused for a second near the top of the screen, where a miniature camera was barely visible. He tucked it in the garland.

“Looks better already. Can you add these?” said Angela, handing him two bows.

“Hey, here’s an idea: What if we use it to show a Yule log?”

“We sell a Treacle Town Yule Log DVD in the gift shop.”

“I’ll download that video and get it going right now.”

Angela beamed and clapped her hands softly. “Yay! It’s all coming together.”

As she paced the lobby, her cell phone at her ear, Angela looked sharp in a crisp white blouse, dark jeans, and patent leather flats. Her glossy hair was tied into a low ponytail with a Christmassy plaid ribbon.

“I got the ideas for the ballroom from Hearst

Castle," Angela said to her mother, who was on the other end of the call. "And the lobby tree was inspired by the Plaza."

Fussing over the décor helped calm her nerves about meeting her mysterious new client, who was scheduled to arrive any minute. She needn't have worried, though: Her amped-up decorations made the inn look like a photo spread from a luxury lifestyle magazine.

Leafy red poinsettias adorned the front desk; a fragrant, oversized wreath hung on the wall behind it; and a majestic Douglas fir, perfectly trimmed in silver, gold, and red ornaments, stood tall in the corner. Mid-morning sun was warming the Saltillo tile floors and reflecting off the delicate decorations.

"I got your picture," Maria said. "Stop fiddling. It's perfect. It's fit for royalty. Or a bunch of sophisticated millionaires."

"Thank you, Mamá! Now wish me luck. The client will be here any second."

Outside the lobby entrance, a lean, statuesque woman had just stepped out of an imposing black SUV. From a distance, Angela had trouble guessing her age, but her posture and attire suggested she was at least in her early fifties.

"Jackson, will you help her with her bags?" Angela said to a chipper staff member. He wheeled a cheerfully decorated bell cart out the doors.

"You must be Angela," the woman said, extending a listless hand mid-stride as she entered the lobby. "I'm Mrs. Lee Glastonbury. Shall we run through our agenda? The others should arrive within a few hours." Despite Angela's snappy appearance, the client looked her up and down as if she were wearing ripped overalls and a crop top.

Lee Glastonbury stood a good three or four inches taller than Angela. She wore tweed slacks, penny loafers, a strand of pearls, and a vintage cashmere twin set. *Seems like something a frugal, old-money dowager would have owned for years and years,* Angela thought—*or exactly the vintage stuff you'd buy if you wanted to imitate such a person.*

Ugh, Bea is getting into my head, Angela told herself. Angela adored Bea, but it sometimes felt like she saw scams around every corner. Angela preferred to believe positive things—and good people—were around the bend.

The client deserved the benefit of the doubt, Angela told herself. She was paying a premium price for an easy event that would even benefit charity. But little suspicions nagged as Angela took in the client's cheap dye job: an unnatural, monotone brown. The color read harsh against her aging skin and sparse brows.

"Why don't we start with the attendee list?" Lee said, peering down at a clipboard in her veiny, crepe-papery hands. "Then I'd like a tour of the facility.

"We've got nine players. You mentioned Ms. Snickerdoodle might like to join, and that would make ten," she began.

"I think she will play."

"Wonderful. More money for our charity. I assume she has the cash on hand now? Not to be pushy—it's for the cause," she was quick to add. "For the prize pool, too, of course. But our players aren't in it for the money. The high stakes simply spark the competitive fires for these super-wealthy men.

"Our players tend to stick with us," Lee continued. "When players drop out, it's usually due to health issues. Well, that's a polite way of saying we've added new players as some of our older ones have passed on—no one seems to leave our game voluntarily. Our new addition this year is Drew Foxworth, a bitcoin investor in his mid-thirties. He heard about our game from the Fischer twins—Rex and Max. They joined a few years ago. The twins made over $100 million investing part of their trust fund in biotech startups. Now they're getting into bitcoin—that's how they met Drew. Apparently, he's been pleading for a while to be included. We don't add people until we know them very well, but the Fischers vouched for Drew. I'll be meeting him for the first time here.

"Eddie Kawai has played for the past seven or eight years. Made his fortune on skateboarding gear and apparel in the 90s. He's well into his fifties now, but you'd never guess it. He's still the same risk-taking lion who manifested that business out of nothing. Important thing to know about him: He's got some severe allergies—that's one of the reasons we wanted to supply the meal ingredients."

"Food allergies are serious business," said Angela. "No wonder you want to be careful. Our chef is very educated on the subject. Food allergies seem common here in Northern California."

"Good. Allergies can be very serious indeed, which is why we're being so cautious," said the client.

"Next we have Walter Wells, the reclusive Sacramento-area property developer. He is a real bear about privacy. He needed to approve our change of location—we were delighted your new inn was available before it opened to the public, to help us avoid attracting unwanted attention.

"The other long-timers value discretion, too—almost above all. Frank Lowell, James Weston, Harry Belmont—they've all been with us since the beginning.

"Harry is our oldest player—he's 63. He's got family money of some sort—he never really explained, and of course no one pressed the matter. Discretion is, as I'm sure you're understanding, our top priority. He's not picky about food, but he's got some dietary concerns, since he's on various medications.

"Frank and James, they're of the same generation—in their late thirties. They made their fortunes in the social media boom. They've known each other since college."

"So, Lee—may I call you Lee?—if I'm counting right, that makes eight. Is there one more?" asked Angela.

"Mrs. Glastonbury, please. I prefer we keep things professional. And, yes, of course you're right. The ninth player is one of our most… interesting characters. Billy Ray Bandy. He has no special food needs, at least none I'm aware of. But keep plenty of his favorite whiskey, Heavenly Mash, on hand."

"We'll send out for some immediately."

"I brought a bottle as part of our bar set-up, and I doubt anyone else will drink much at all. The others will want to stay sharp for the poker games. But best to get a couple more bottles for the rest of our stay."

"With the money involved, I assumed there wouldn't be much drinking."

"Well, perhaps it's different when you're playing with your wife's money—but you didn't hear that from me," Mrs. Glastonbury said tartly. "Billy Ray's wife's family money just happens to come from Heavenly Mash Distillery. So I suppose at least his habit puts some money back in their coffers. But in any case, I doubt Mr. Bandy believes his drinking affects his play."

"Isn't Heavenly Mash one of those liquor companies that started before Prohibition?"

"I believe so, yes. Storied history. Perhaps you can ask his wife to share a bit of the saga."

"What's Mr. Bandy's wife's name?"

"Connie. Connie Hollander. You don't read the society pages, I guess," Lee added, with a touch of disdain. "She's going by Connie Bandy now."

"That reminds me to ask, will the other players bring their wives? Just wanting to be sure we set up properly for breakfast."

"Sometimes, one or two bring a female companion. We don't ask about those relationships—and I expect your staff to use the same discretion. It won't affect the room count, I assure you. And, frankly, I doubt the companions will show up at breakfast, although it can't hurt to plan for an extra person or two. Now, let's move on to the facility tour."

"Of course," said Angela, turning toward the ballroom as the sound of a roaring engine grabbed their attention. An exotic car—a gleaming, lipstick-red machine—zoomed into the driveway. Angela leaned toward the lobby doors to get a peek at its driver: a rangy, broad-shouldered man who was now striding into the lobby.

"Lee!" the man called, extending his hand smoothly toward Mrs. Glastonbury. "You're Lee Glastonbury, right? Drew Foxworth. How are you? You suggested we players arrive later today, but I decided I'd show up a little early, get comfortable, relax a little."

With latte-colored skin, close-cropped black hair, and a neat goatee, Drew Foxworth was head-turningly handsome. He wore jeans, driving moccasins, a boldly colored fitted shirt—and a look of unshakeable confidence. Angela cracked a discreet smile when she saw Lee wince at his informality.

Despite his smarm, there was something magnetic about Drew Foxworth.

"There's no reason you can't enjoy the afternoon here," she replied, seeming uncomfortable. "We're going to do a walk-through of the event space."

"Great!" he enthused. "I'll join you if you don't mind." Angela saw Lee open her mouth to say she did, but Drew continued, undaunted.

"Now Lee, who is this ravishing creature?" he gushed while cradling Angela's right hand in both of his. "Why have you been holding out on me, Lee? You didn't mention any women when you walked me through the player list."

"She's not a player, Drew. She runs the inn. Her name is Angela Garcia."

Still holding her hand, Drew turned to face Angela, who hoped her makeup concealed the flush spreading across her cheeks and neck.

"Beautiful and accomplished, too. Lovely to meet you, Angela. As you heard, my name's Drew Foxworth—but I hope you'll call me Foxy. All my friends do."

His almond-shaped, dark-brown eyes were looking into hers with an awkward intensity. His perfect teeth stood straight and sparkling. A little voice in Angela's head warned her intellect not to be too dazzled by his buttery swagger, but the rest of her was paying zero attention.

"OK, well, nice to meet you, Foxy—er, Mr. Foxworth. Shall we all head to the ballroom? Mrs. Glastonbury, I'm looking forward to showing you the set-up for tonight."

As Angela led the way down the hall, she made a point of focusing on her client, even as Foxy kept trying to divert her attention. She was determined to meet Lee Glastonbury's demanding expectations, starting with a great first impression.

She opened the large center doors of the inn's ballroom and revealed the opulent, classic holiday décor she'd put so much energy into designing. Angela noticed with relief that her client seemed to relax once she saw the space and recognized that preparations for the evening's event were well in hand. Though the expansive ballroom was big enough for events many times bigger than Lee's, the furniture was arranged in a focused way in one section of the room, creating an unexpected sense of coziness. Christmas trees, a bar area, and conversational seating areas helped fill some of the extra space. Perry was there, arranging luxurious leather chairs around two freshly re-felted poker tables—the focal point of the event.

"Mrs. Glastonbury, this is Perry James, professional tournament director."

"Nice to meet you, Perry. Poker set-up looks good. We won't need those, though," she added, pointing to the sealed packages of tournament poker chips and Christmas-themed card decks on the table. "We always provide our own."

"Of course," Perry replied neutrally.

"Too bad," said Drew, picking up a deck and examining the design. "They've got a lot of holiday spirit."

"With so much money at stake, I'm sure you can understand why we want to keep a tight rein on all aspects of the game. I consider it my personal responsibility."

"Well, then, thank you for watching out for us players, Lee," Drew said.

Perry pointed up towards the ceiling in the corner of the ballroom. "I'm sure you're interested in security. Note the small camera. The door it sits above goes to the control room—where there's a safe for storing cash and chips."

"Excellent."

Drew walked up toward the control room for a better view of the camera. "Looks modern. Can I get a peek at the server and the safe?"

"Door's locked at the moment. No one here

has a fingerprint with access," Perry replied. "Aseem will be here shortly. He's our tech expert."

"Drew, I'll confirm the security is all in order before we get started. You have my word," Lee Glastonbury said, eying him suspiciously. "You're new to our event, but players have entrusted security to me for years because I couldn't be more particular about it if it were my own money. Perry, can I count on you to show me the full set-up once Aseem arrives?"

"Of course."

"We'll also have an elegantly dressed guard at the door," Angela chimed in.

"Thank you. An atmosphere that projects both security and exclusivity is very important to us."

"Oh yes, that reminds me… with only a few hours now until your event begins, perhaps we should go get ready—assuming you've seen enough, I mean. I've engaged a hair and makeup specialist—you're more than welcome to join me and Bea."

"That sounds lovely. But one more thing, Angela. You haven't mentioned room assignments yet. I'd like to be sure my room is as close as possible to the ballroom—for convenience," she added quickly.

"I hadn't considered that. But we can make a

quick change. Let's head to the front desk right now."

"Good. And I can review all the room assignments and locations, if you don't mind."

"Not at all," said Angela, though she wondered why the room assignments would matter so much. All the suites were similar in size and furnishings.

"I'd like to be close to the ballroom, too," piped up Foxy. "Next closest after Lee chooses her room, of course. Would that be OK with you, Lee? I prefer being close to the action."

"By all means," said Lee, with forced agreeableness.

"Great! So I guess we'll all head back to the front desk together. Lead the way, gorgeous Angela."

CHAPTER 5

Angela stopped off at Bea's suite on the way back to her own. She was carrying a large box—a package she'd been anxiously waiting for.

She found the door ajar at Bea's suite—and a curious conversation underway inside.

"See what I mean?" Bea was saying. "They're not just rude, they're incredibly stupid—and they look to me like they were all written by the same person. See? All posted on the same day."

"Looks like we're dealing with a type of troll," said Pat. "Trolls can be tough, though. They're usually good at covering their tracks. Requires a lot of monitoring and luck to catch 'em in the act."

"A troll! I love it!" said Bea. "We're up for the challenge. Operation Troll Patrol is underway.

How do you like my code name? It'll help us keep our project a secret, like real detective—"

"Knock-knock," said Angela, pushing the door open and entering the suite. "OK if I come in?"

"Oh hi, Angie!" Bea squeaked. She yanked the computer's power cord out of the socket, forgetting that the laptop had battery power. The web page she'd hoped to conceal remained brightly displayed on the screen. She tried unsuccessfully to block it with her diminutive frame.

"Angie, this is Pat—Pat Rogers, you recall, the private eye from Charlie's building. Pat, meet Angela; Angela, Pat," Bea said, simultaneously lowering the laptop screen behind her back.

"Hi Pat, nice to meet you in person," Angela said, tossing the big box on the bed and peering around Bea to get a look at the laptop. "Bea, isn't that the sales page for Betty's last book? Were those reviews on that screen? And what's this talk of a 'code name'?"

"Nothing to worry about, Angie," Bea said. She shot a warning glance in Pat's direction.

"Why do I sense you two are up to something —something to do with those reviews? Bea, may I remind you we agreed that I would deal with any negative reviews—and that besides, the only appropriate response to any reviewer is a respectful 'thank you'?"

"You might not want to say 'thank you' if you saw these!" blurted Pat.

"Now, now, Angela. You don't need to worry," interrupted Bea, glaring at Pat. "Pat and I are just having fun. We're not planning anything related to reviews that may or may not have recently appeared for Betty's ebooks. What's in your box, girlie?"

"Bea, this discussion isn't over, OK? We can put a pin in it until after our big event. In the meantime, I assume we're on the same page about not responding to reviews. If there's any reason I shouldn't assume that—"

"Consider it assumed," said Bea. "Now, let's see what's in this chichi box you've brought me."

"OK, let's see if you like this," Angela said, lifting the lid of the extravagant box and pulling back clouds of pretty tissue. "I just thought you might like something new, to help you meet our black tie optional requirements. I mean, only if you want to wear it. Fancy... but I still hope you'll like it."

She held up a charcoal gray top that was soft like a comfortable jersey, but was covered in delicate sequins hand-sewn in a beautiful pattern.

"It's easy as anything you'd normally wear, but still dressy. There are black silk pull-on pants to go with it—just as comfortable as sweats—and more tops and pants for the other nights."

"Aw, thanks, Angie!" said Bea. "These will go great with my black sheepskin boots. I did some shopping myself, but I didn't find anything this good."

Angela shuddered to think about what Bea chose for semi-formal attire on her own. What a relief that her gift had passed the test. The outfits weren't quite "black tie," but she doubted it was possible to get Bea any more dressed up.

"The hair and makeup expert will arrive in a couple hours. I invited Mrs. Glastonbury—Lee—to join us."

"'Mrs. Glastonbury?' Sounds hoity-toity. What's she like? The curiosity is killing me."

"You'll have a chance to decide for yourself," Angela said. "Hair and makeup will be at my suite at 5:00. Bring your new outfit to change into. We'll go straight to the ballroom after. Pat, did Bea tell you about our black-tie event?"

"I might have forgotten to mention it," Bea said. "Sorry, Pat, I didn't know about it yet when I invited you. Could you borrow one of these outfits?"

"Oh yeah, great idea, Bea," Pat chuckled, picking up a pair of Bea's new pants and squeezing her arm inside one leg. "Fits like a glove—literally. Don't worry, though—I've got the perfect solution. Just wait a minute and I'll show you."

Pat left through the interior door that led to her adjoining suite. Moments later, she burst back through it.

"Ta-da!" she said, doing a model's twirl. "It's my P.I. secret weapon. I never travel without it."

"Close your mouth, girlie," Bea chortled, elbowing Angela. "The whole world can see your tonsils!"

Pat's secret weapon was a beige uniform of stiff khakis and a matching shirt. The ill-fitting outfit seemed to have lopped half a foot off Pat's height—and added it right onto her hips. Massive black combat boots completed the look.

"Those boots are delightful," cackled Bea. "I'm surprised you can lift your feet. Were you planning to take a hike through nuclear waste? "Suggest you loosen that big belt, though. You look like a mealbag tied in the middle," Bea continued, guffawing and slapping her knee over and over.

"Bea!" Angela gasped. She didn't actually know what a "mealbag" might be, but she was pretty sure Bea's comment was an insult.

"Don't worry, Miss Garcia," said Pat. "I'm grateful for constructive criticism from such a well-known fashion icon."

"Good one, Pat," said Angela.

"Respect," said Bea, nodding and holding her gnarled fist up to Pat's for a bump.

"This outfit isn't about looking good. It's about fitting in anywhere I want. I just pass as a security guard. It's handy for any situation where I want to nose around," Pat said. "It's the kind of thing you should start thinking about, Bea, since you want to learn how to be a detective."

"Wait, what?" said Angela. "Somebody's learning to be a detective?"

"Nobody, Angie. I thought it would be fun to learn what detecting's like. You know I told you how I found something to do over Christmas—before we had our big client. That's what it was—I wanted a detective course designed for a curious layperson. That's why I invited Pat." Bea waited until she thought Angela wasn't looking, then shot Pat a look of exasperation.

"It can't hurt to have another security guard at our fat-cat tournament tonight, though—right, Angie? Pat could play security guard but keep her eyes open for real—assuming you don't mind, Pat."

"Works for me," Pat said. "But I assume one of you will tell me what the event's all about?"

"I suppose we can't have too much security," Angela replied. "Why don't you fill Pat in on our high-roller situation before we get our hair and makeup done? I'm going to go figure out what to wear. See you at 5:00."

"Good gravy, I thought she'd never leave!" Bea said as she closed the door behind Angela.

"I guess I neglected to tell you a few important details, Pat. Angela can't find out what we're up to with those reviews! You saw for yourself how particular and straight-laced she is. She doesn't want me posting replies, but who knows what we'll find when we start digging? What if we want to cook up some way to respond without replying? She might not like that, either, so let's not give her a chance to react. Operation Troll Patrol is just between us, OK?"

"Got it."

"Ditto for the detective thing and *especially* the mystery writing. She'll get all nervous that I'll kill Betty the Golden Goose. The timing's gotta be just right when I tell her."

"No problemo."

"You know what else? Your security guard getup could come in handy. I've been thinking that this high-roller poker event might turn out to be an even bigger mystery than those reviews. My gut says it's not entirely kosher, but I can't figure out what they're up to. Since I'll be busy playing, I can use your extra eyes and ears."

"Sounds like fun," Pat said. "And here you were mocking my getup. I'm dressed just right for hiding in plain sight."

ANGELA'S SUITE was on the other end of the inn, so she often preferred to walk the grounds instead of taking the interior hallways. She couldn't get enough of the stunning landscape of the ranch, its wide-open, rolling green acres dotted here and there with mature trees. There was a field of dormant grapevines across the road, and vineyards and wineries on either side of the property, all providing beautiful boundaries. The air was crisp and the winter light had a peaceful, golden cast.

As she walked, Angela considered Lee Glastonbury. Angela hadn't been around family money enough to guess whether the woman's regal attitude and low-key appearance were genuine artifacts. But could they be too spot-on—as if Lee came out of central casting?

Shoot! I forgot to ask for details about the charity.

Wasn't it weird, though, that Mrs. Glastonbury had volunteered almost nothing about it?

Whether she was a real Brahmin or a skilled faker, the woman put Angela on edge—as did the pressure of meeting the expectations of the millionaire players. These people were used to having the best of everything. She hated the prospect of missing the mark in even the tiniest way.

Back at her suite, Angela opened the door and caught her breath—then laughed. Though she hadn't ordered anything for herself, a large box, a bigger and grander version of the one she'd brought Bea, sat on her bed.

A card was tucked under the huge satin bow on top of the box:

"I'm sure you were planning to wear that little black dress of yours. You always look great, but shouldn't our company president make a bold statement? See what you think of these."

Angela lifted the lid and found, under billows of tissue, an outfit wrapped in electric blue paper. She peeled the wrapping to reveal a shocking tube top in a neon animal print and a hot pink leatherette miniskirt.

Very funny, Bea. But then she noticed something else: another note tucked in the pocket of the eye-searing pink skirt.

"Hahaha girlie! Just kidding. Save that getup for when I drag you to the cardroom for poker. You'll distract all the fish and we'll clean up! Keep looking, there's more underneath."

Beneath more tissue Angela found three gorgeous dresses.

The first was a knockout: a long-sleeved sheath covered in black sequins and tiny, light-catching beads—understated and refined in shape, but with a sexy low back.

The second was equally stunning. A gold metallic halter dress with a cinched waist, it had loose waves of a mysterious, soft fabric that draped to just above the knee.

When Angela pulled the last one out, though, she couldn't stop smiling. "This is it. I'll wear this tonight."

It was a sweet but chic sleeveless dress made of gorgeous midnight blue silk taffeta. Under its nipped-in waist was a flouncy skirt with a light crinoline.

"It's perfect!" she proclaimed as she modeled it

for herself in the mirror. The dress had just the right amount of sex appeal to put a spring in her step—as did the gorgeous black velvet stilettos that were also in the box. Angela found them inexplicably cloud-like when she slipped them on.

She took off the dress and hung it inside the bathroom. She turned on the hot water in the shower to steam out a few small wrinkles in the silk.

In her bathrobe, while waiting for the shower to do its magic, she fired up her computer for a quick scan of those reviews Bea had been determined to conceal. She frowned as she saw the same mean comments Bea had.

The Treacle Town series had scarcely received a negative comment in a review before, much less a one-star rating. The books were written for people who loved sweet stories of love and the holidays—and they hit their mark perfectly. Yet it seemed that people who'd never enjoy a sweet Christmas romance in the first place were dinging Betty's latest for being what it promised.

Or possibly not "people," but person: just as Bea had, Angela noticed the odd similarity of the trashy reviews.

Just what I need, she thought—*a marketing mess and no time to figure out what to do about it. No chance Bea and Pat would stop digging, either, or planning some kind of retaliation.* If there was one thing Bea could never, ever resist, it was dishing out well-deserved smack-down.

Angela sighed. No point in worrying about it now. Thank goodness the millionaire games would keep those two occupied for the night, where she could keep an eye on them—along with all the moving parts of their luxe event.

CHAPTER 6

The four ladies—Angela, Bea, Lee, and Pat—made their way from Angela's suite back to the ballroom. The beauty treatments seemed to have perked them all up (except perhaps for Pat, who hadn't partaken and had just come along for company).

Angela was particularly chipper, thanks both to being all dolled up and the thrilling sensation she was pulling off her first VIP event.

They walked two-abreast heading to the ballroom, Angela next to Bea, towering over her thanks to the new heels. "I'm as tall as Mrs. Glastonbury now," Angela whispered, leaning down towards Bea's ear. "I can look her right in the eye, even when she's talking down to me."

Bea snorted, a little too loudly. The client looked back at them, trying to figure out what she'd overheard.

A few steps later, Bea caught Angela's attention and mouthed "We need to talk—in private!" Angela nodded.

Bea reached up and swiped her hand across Angela's mouth. Her finger left a trail of red lipstick from Angela's lips to her chin.

"Hey!" hissed Angela.

"Angie, you look so pretty, but you smeared your lipstick," Bea announced in a loud, stilted voice.

"Oh, I didn't know I smeared it," Angela replied, equally oafishly. "What should I do?"

"Let's just stop in my suite and fix it," Bea said. "We're just about to walk by it."

"Good idea. Pat, would you mind accompanying Mrs. Glastonbury to the ballroom? It would be helpful to have your reassuring presence there right from the start, anyway."

"Sure, Angela. Why do you think I got all duded up in my best uniform?" Pat said.

Angela stood by the mirror in Bea's bathroom and repaired her face. "Sheesh, what a mess, Bea. Good thing I had my lipstick in my pocket. So, let's hear it, what's your opinion of Mrs. Glastonbury?"

"She's a puzzle, all right," Bea said. "Still not onto her game, but give me time."

"Do we have to assume there's a scam involved? I see why you're suspicious—I do—but isn't it possible she's just pushy and demanding?"

"Not a matter of either/or, Angie," snorted Bea.

"She didn't say much during our manicures. It seemed a little rude," Angela admitted. "But I don't know any old-money people. Maybe that's just how they are."

"Rude? I'd say more likely shrewd. I bet she was hoping I'd reveal something. She was sizing me up, just like I was her."

"Did it seem to you she was faking her old-money image?"

"I dunno. Too bad you couldn't run her pearls over your teeth."

"Honestly, Bea. Where do you come up with your crazy ideas? That's gross."

"That's how you tell if pearls are real. If they're rough, they're real."

"Interesting, but I doubt I'll have an opportunity to stick her necklace in my mouth. Anyway, she told you about some of your poker competitors. That was at least nice, wasn't it?"

"Yeah, really useful information—not. In case

you're wondering later, Frank's the one with the sideburns, Harry's the old quiet guy, Walter's the next oldest, and Billy Ray's the good ole boy. That's some high-level intelligence. And she still told us nothing about her 'charity,'" Bea said, making exaggerated air quotes with her knobbly fingers.

"So what do we do?" Angela sighed.

"Just keep our wits about us, girlie. And be glad we already got that $25K deposit."

"There's something else I wanted to tell you. I met one player, Drew Foxworth. Goes by 'Foxy.' He kept asking about the security for the tournament. He was getting under Mrs. Glastonbury's skin. And they both made a big deal about having rooms right near the ballroom."

"Foxy?" snorted Bea. "Oh, brother."

"Mrs. Glastonbury insisted on reviewing the rooms. She said some of the players were picky about whose rooms were next door. Foxy seemed very interested where the other players' rooms would be, too, but Mrs. Glastonbury eventually nudged him to get his key and move along while she assigned the rest."

"Sounds like he's another one for us to keep an eye on."

"You look pretty, Bea."

"Oh no! I hope not too pretty. I don't want my good looks to interfere with my doddering old hag routine."

"Uh-oh. You might have to fall back on skill," Angela said, smiling.

"The old hag routine *is* my skill. Better wish me luck, girlie."

ANGELA SURVEYED the ballroom with satisfaction. Everything looked just right.

The servers and bartender wore black tuxedo pants, white tuxedo shirts, and red plaid cummerbunds and bow ties. The dealers were similarly dressed, but their cummerbunds and ties were dark green.

Perry, who was sharing last-minute instructions with the dealers, was dressed like them, except with a tuxedo jacket on top. The slight smile on his craggy face conveyed confidence and experience. His salt-and-pepper hair was neatly combed. Pat was standing guard at the door, looking strong and official in her all-purpose security guard outfit.

"Pat, have you seen Aseem?" Angela asked Pat.

"He's inside the control room. He said he's just

double-checking the video set-up. Then he'll open up the safe for the games and stand guard outside the open door to make sure only you or Perry have access."

Angela tilted her head and saw Aseem working on the monitor beside the safe. "Perfect. I should have known that's where he'd be."

Elegantly dressed guests were now arriving. Everyone seemed to enjoy the dignified yet festive atmosphere.

Angela walked toward Lee Glastonbury, who was standing beside one of Angela's splendid Christmas trees. The client's red silk gown and matching bolero jacket sat slightly off the shoulder, exposing a little skin. A suitable choice, Angela thought, for a moneyed matriarch.

"Does everything meet your expectations so far, Mrs. Glastonbury?"

"How could it not?" declared Drew Foxworth, who appeared out of nowhere and draped his arm around Angela's shoulder in a proprietary fashion. "Everything here looks almost as beautiful as you. I'm impressed."

"It's Mrs. Glastonbury's event, Mr. Foxworth. All I'm doing is executing it to her specifications," Angela said. Mrs. Glastonbury was appraising his perfectly fitted midnight blue tuxedo with irritation. To Angela, Foxy looked... foxy. But his bold choice seemed to have the opposite effect on her fussy client.

"C'mon, Lee, admit it. It's great, right? At least tell Angela you appreciate her hard work."

Mrs. Glastonbury looked away from him and addressed Angela. "Let's confer before my introduction, just before the games start." Then she walked away to join another group of guests.

"Well, that went well," Angela giggled, smiling up at Foxy's handsome face. Inner alarm bells warned her not to, but she couldn't help enjoying his flattering attention. "Excuse me, Mr. Foxworth, I'd better be sure she's not displeased." She ducked out from under his arm and started to walk away. "Good luck in the tournament."

"She's fine. And please, enough of that 'Mr. Foxworth' nonsense. Call me Foxy," Foxy said, deftly moving his arm back around Angela's shoulders and guiding her the other way, toward the bar. "Look at us, a matched set in midnight blue. It's like we belong together. Walk with me to get a beverage."

"OK, sure, Mr.—er, Foxy," Angela said. "But just for a moment. I've got work to do."

"I understand. Perhaps later you can give me a tour of the inn and the grounds? I'd love to learn more about the business. I don't know much about hospitality."

"Frankly, I'm just getting started myself. I'm more of a marketer by trade—but I'm learning. I'd like to know about your business, too. Bitcoin, right?"

"You've done your homework. Impressive."

After half a glass of champagne and a full dose of Foxy's charm, Angela was giggling coquettishly. All the cautions she'd repeated to herself earlier were thrown to the wind.

From his post in front of the control room, Aseem tried to get her attention. He had an urgent expression on his face, but she waved him off. She held up one finger, then turned back to Foxy—soon becoming so engrossed again that she didn't even notice Bea walking straight toward her.

"Angela, may I have a word?"

"Is this your granny, beautiful?" Drew said, more charm dripping from his pillowy lips. "Drew Foxworth," he added, extending a hand toward Bea. "But my friends call me Foxy."

"Hahaha, Foxy, good one. I bet some people say that's a girl's nickname, but who cares? I say you wear it well."

Angela shot Bea a mortified glance, which Bea ignored.

"I'm Bea, but all my favorite people call me Betty. Betty Snickerdoodle. My name's on the door of this joint. Angela tells me you're one of the poker players. I hope you won't play too tough on an old lady like me."

"You play? I hope you're not a shark. I'm new to the game myself," Foxy said. His patronizing tone suggested he was on deck to join the large ranks of poker players who regretted underestimating Bea.

"Me? A shark? That's rich!" Bea laughed, slapping her knee reflexively. "Angela's always saying I've got more money than brains. Isn't that right, Angie? I'm just a dumb romance author who got lucky and hit it big. Now that I've got all the cash, I'll try anything once. I heard about the tournament and couldn't resist giving it a go. Granny ain't getting any younger, right? I got that thing you young people call foaming."

"Foaming?" said Angela.

"You know, when you're sad because everyone else is having fun right under your nose."

"FOMO?" smirked Foxy. "Fear of missing out?"

"Hahaha, I guess that's it, Foxy," guffawed Bea, giving her knee another good smack. "See what I mean? I'm half out of marbles. But don't you worry about me. I just want to have fun and get my little taste of the high-roller life—and believe me, I can afford it. Besides, it's for a good charity, right?"

I bet that's what she's up to, Angela thought. *She's trying to get the lowdown on that charity. Or she's priming the pump to take Foxy's money. More likely both. That foaming thing was clearly an act—but Foxy seemed none the wiser. Bea always says that an old lady can get away with virtually any lie, as long as she's playing dumb.*

"I'm mainly here for the poker, Betty. Lee didn't tell me much about the charity at all. Something about children. Rex and Max—the Fischer twins—have been telling me about the game for a while now, and it sounded like a lot of fun. But we've hardly talked about the charity."

"Guess it's just a clever way to nudge us richie-riches to do our part, huh?" said Bea, punching Foxy on the bicep. "Ooh, someone's been working out!" She pinched the underside of his muscular arm in a manner that bordered on groping. "What do you think, Angie, could we break away for that word?"

Angela cringed with embarrassment, but her face lit up again when Foxy winked at her. Bea grabbed her hand and pulled her away.

"See you at the table, Foxy," Bea said. "I'm

looking forward to learning a thing or two about poker from you!"

"I'm looking forward to seeing *you* later, gorgeous Angela," said Foxy. Angela could have sworn a little twinkle of light glinted off one of his perfect incisors.

"Girlie, get a grip," said Bea, once they were out of Foxy's earshot. Angela was still looking in Foxy's direction, beaming.

"I know, I know. Don't worry, I'm not taking it seriously. It's just harmless fun to flirt a little."

"I wonder if Aseem would think it's harmless."

"That's no business of his now, is it? We're friends. Despite your insinuations, he's never acted like anything but."

"If you say so," Bea snorted. "But I hope you're not forgetting we're supposed to be keeping an eye on Foxy—not getting hypnotized by him."

"Don't you think I can keep an eye on him a whole lot better if I let him flirt with me?"

"Just keep your brain turned on. I think you're getting a little googly-eyed. And speaking of Aseem, he just told me something about Mr. Foxy Foxworth that I think you should hear. He's been trying to tell you himself."

"What's that?"

"He said that while he was setting up the video

in the control room, Lee Glastonbury came in to ask questions—and Foxy tagged along. He said both of them were digging for details—Foxy in particular. Aseem explained what you said—that proper security requires that we limit access to our controlled areas. But Foxy still pressed for details of the set-up."

"Couldn't he just be concerned because his buy-in's so big?"

"The buy-in's big, girlie—bigger than I've ever seen—but I've also never once seen a tournament player demand to inspect the video surveillance set-up."

"OK, OK. Duly noted. I promise to keep my eyes open about Foxy. It looks Mrs. Glastonbury is getting ready to speak. I'll make sure she doesn't need any help from me before we get started."

"You take care of her, and I'll make sure Perry and the dealers are all set, too."

Angela tapped a water goblet and asked everyone to give Mrs. Glastonbury their attention.

"Thank you all for joining us for our annual Christmas event. First, let's welcome our new player, Drew Foxworth." The players applauded. Foxy smiled at Mrs. Glastonbury and ostentatiously raised his champagne glass in her direction.

"And welcome back to the rest of the players and your guests. I hope you've been enjoying Betty Snickerdoodle's delightful inn so far—I know I have been."

Angela blushed as Foxy interrupted Mrs. Glastonbury to applaud and announce, "And cheers to Angela!"

"Most of you no doubt remember our tournament rules," continued Mrs. Glastonbury. "But just in case, a refresher. At the table, we follow the standard rules of the tournament directors' association in the United States. In case you need it, you were all emailed a link.

"Second, as is our convention, you've all bought in for three nights of single-table tournaments. In the event you decide to—or need to—withdraw before the tournaments are concluded, your buy-in remains in the prize pool. In other words, no refunds.

"We'll play one-hour levels, to reduce the influence of luck. We'll use the big-blind ante format starting at level ten. That means instead of all players posting an ante, the player in the big blind will post all of them as part of the blind bet. This way, the dealer won't have to wait for everyone to count out their ante before starting the hand.

"Remember, please plan to stay all three nights, because all of our prizes are awarded at our traditional goodbye breakfast after the third night's tournament."

"That rule didn't work out so great for that guy who died last time," blurted one of the players, laughing sarcastically.

Foxy cocked his head and studied the man's face. Harry and Walter scowled like annoyed grown-ups in the company of an obnoxious teenager, a slight sheen forming on Harry's bald head. The twins looked shocked.

"Just a joke, people," he continued. "Ain't like he can hear it!"

Angela hadn't met the man yet. But his ruddy cheeks and mountain twang, plus the whiskey in his hand, gave her the impression he must be Billy Ray Bandy. The timid-looking woman standing next to him, holding a pretty little dachshund, must be Connie, his wife.

"Finally," continued Mrs. Glastonbury, "I'd like to introduce you to our tournament director, Perry James. His decisions on questions of the game will be final."

Perry nodded, acknowledging the introduction.

"I trust that, with our tradition of cordiality, disputes will be unlikely. You're all fine gentlemen, after all. Oh, that reminds me—for the first time, we have a woman joining in the action. I hope you've all met her—she's the lady whose name is on this lovely inn. Let's impress her with our refined and sportsmanlike style of poker."

Angela exchanged a quick grin with Perry. She suspected he was thinking the same thing she was: "refined style" was unlikely to impress Bea.

"Oh, come *on,* Lee," interrupted Billy Ray. "Can't we just get started already? Let us play, for the love of Pete! We ain't getting any younger—you especially."

"Let the game begin," said Lee, with concealed irritation. "Perry, let's shuffle up and deal."

CHAPTER 7

By midnight, all but four players—Eddie Kawai, Billy Ray Bandy, Frank Lowell, and James Weston—had been knocked out of the tournament. Harry Belmont had just been eliminated and was standing by the bar, sipping a nightcap. Foxy, the twins, and Walter Wells were playing in the high-stakes side game. The atmosphere was jovial and relaxed, despite the hundred-dollar bills stacked on the table.

Rex and Max, the Nordic-looking twins, were accompanied by gorgeous, gazelle-like twin women. The ladies wore identical emerald-green slip dresses and draped themselves like accessories on the shoulders of their dates. They had blank expressions on their flawless faces and long, shiny, stick-straight hair parted in the middle.

"I just figured out how I recognize Rex and Max's dates," Angela whispered to Bea. "They're those famous twin runway models."

"The four of them look like the envoys of a super race sent to mesmerize Earthlings and take over our planet," Bea snickered.

"I'd love to look like those models do," Angela sighed.

"That's nuts, girlie," said Bea. "You're at least as pretty as those giraffes."

"Even in these heels, I feel like a tree stump next to them."

"Why would you compare yourself to some rich guys' human accessories? Do I need to remind you you're running this place? They're spectators in the boys' game, and you're running the table in your own."

"Thanks, Bea. That's sweet," Angela smiled.

"I mean it. Can't you see how well your event is going? It's so fun that even those empty-headed Barbies are staying up late. We gotta work on your confidence."

"Any thoughts on who'll win?" Angela said, stifling a yawn. "It has turned into a marathon."

"Billy Ray's got to be driving them nuts," Bea

said. "He's like the thing that wouldn't leave. A terrible player and half-plastered to boot. He's been on the verge of busting at least half a dozen times and has sucked out every time."

"Look at his poor wife," said Angela.

Connie Bandy sat behind her husband, looking like she had trouble keeping her eyes open. An hour earlier, she'd said she wanted to head to their suite to go to bed. But Billy Ray had insisted—harshly—that she had to stay "so his luck wouldn't turn bad." The tiny copper-colored dog on her lap had given in to sleepiness and was snoring softly.

"Ooh, I think that little dog of hers is the most darling creature I've ever seen," said Angela.

"Ha!" whispered Bea. "You used to think that about Aseem, until Smarmy McSuave turned your head." Angela rolled her eyes and sighed.

"We've got an all-in and a call," announced the tournament dealer. Someone was about to either bust out of the tournament or double their chips.

Billy Ray was all in again, this time against Eddie Kawai—the biggest stack at the table. Billy Ray stood up and flipped his cards over defiantly: the ace of clubs and the nine of hearts.

"Thanks for the action," Billy Ray slurred to Eddie, sneering. He was using the table to steady himself, causing the chip stacks to wobble. His tuxedo shirt was partly untucked and his floppy Western bow tie was half-undone and dangling.

"You're welcome," Eddie replied, turning over two red kings.

"Oh boy," Bea said to Angela. "It's looking bad for Billy Ray. But he's gotten his money in worse than that and been saved by the deck. I'm sure the others are hoping Eddie's hand holds up. It's annoying to play with loudmouth drunks. Time for Billy Ray to hit the hay."

"I got outs!" shouted Billy Ray. "Gimme an ace, dealer!"

The dealer discarded a burn card and began to spread the flop—the first three of the five community cards Billy Ray and Eddie would combine with their two cards to form their best hand. Connie's wee dog woke with a start and let out a little yelp, as if she'd had a bad dream, just as the dealer placed Billy Ray's nightmare card on the board: the king of spades. Billy Ray's chances of staying in the game had just evaporated.

"Where's my ace, dealer?" Billy Ray shouted.

"He's drawing dead and doesn't even realize it," said Bea.

"Drawing dead?" said Angela.

"There's no card in the deck that can help him."

The light finally turned on in Billy Ray's

drunken head, and he realized Bea was right just as the dealer placed the next card. Billy Ray's rude impatience became fury. He reached over and grabbed the dachshund's little face, which was no larger than the palm of his hand. Without warning, he reached his arm back and swung it at the tiny dog's face.

Bea and Angela gasped. The dog recoiled and Billy Ray missed, his arm whooshing past her face. Losing her balance on Connie's lap, the pooch fell onto the floor and peed herself with fright.

"Oh Bijou, I'm sorry!" Connie cried, reaching down to soothe her pet, who was now hiding under her chair, behind the hem of her pink satin gown. "Daddy didn't mean it!"

"Course I meant it," said Billy Ray. "Stupid bitch ruined my luck. I told you not to bring her. Somebody get me another Heavenly Mash."

Bea caught the bartender's eye and made the cut sign under her neck, while Angela bent down to see if the pup was OK. The bartender hurried over with a towel to mop up the floor. The dealer placed the fifth and final card onto the board, though it was immaterial to the outcome. No mathematical miracle this time: Billy Ray was out.

"Finally," whispered Bea to Perry. "Let's hope he doesn't want to play in the cash game. The way he's behaving, he's on the verge of ruining Angela's big night."

"Never mind the drink. Stupid game's rigged, anyway," Billy Ray bellowed, cursing and almost knocking his vacant chair over. "Of course one of Lee's little favorites is going to win. Always seems to happen. Cheers to you, Skateboard King."

Perry put a hand on the dealer's shoulder and told her to pause the game, then walked to the tournament clock and stopped it.

Lee Glastonbury seemed worried about her glamorous night being ruined, too. She hurried to the table and placed an arm on Billy Ray's shoulder, hoping to quiet him. "Just bad luck. It'll be better tomorrow—"

"Save it, Lee. I meant what I said. You might fool everyone else, but not me. Can't wait to see the seat assignments tomorrow—if I decide to come back and play."

Bea's eyes opened a little wider. She noticed that Perry's did, too.

"I'm sure you'll feel better in the morning," Lee insisted. "It will be a whole new game and a whole new seating arrangement."

"Yeah, we'll see. Connie, let's go—now. And find someplace else for that mutt to sleep tonight."

"But Billy Ray, where—" stammered Connie.

"Your problem, woman. I don't want to see that hound in our suite tonight!"

Other than Connie's barely audible crying, the room fell silent—everyone frozen, wondering what would happen next.

"I'll take her," Angela blurted. "Bijou can stay with me."

"Good, now let's get out of here, Connie—now!" shouted Billy Ray, grabbing his wife's arm. Connie looked back at Angela and Bijou with concern.

"It's OK, she'll be fine," said Angela, picking up the dog, looping her leash in her hand. "I'll take her out for a little walk, then bring her back to my suite."

Bea watched Angela follow Billy Ray and Connie out the doors of the ballroom. Connie looked back to mouth an anxious "thank you" to Angela.

"Lee—Mrs. Glastonbury—I hope you're not concerned about Billy Ray's outburst," Foxy said kindly. "It's obvious he's just had too much to drink." This deferential Foxy seemed to Bea a different man than the relentless charm machine she'd seen working on Angela earlier in the evening.

"You and I have got plenty to talk about," Bea whispered to Perry.

"Indeed. Bet you're curious as I am to see how this plays out," Perry replied, flipping the tournament clock back on.

"OK dealer," Perry announced. "Put the cards back in the air."

"Don't worry about what Billy Ray said. It's still anyone's game, right?" Eddie said to his opponents, seemingly trying to restore the festive mood. "Anything can happen at a poker table!"

CHAPTER 8

Two hours of civilized play later, Eddie Kawai had extended his chip lead to more than half of the chips in play in the tournament. James had about double the stack of Frank, who was running low on chips. Momentum on his side, Eddie was breaking away to the finish. The side game had slowed down, with Foxy and Walter getting up frequently to stretch their legs and observe the progress of the tournament. Rex and Max's dates had already headed back to their suites for the night, as had Harry.

"Too bad we can't chop the prize," said Eddie. "I'd be happy to split it, even though I have the biggest stack by far. Who knew we'd be playing so long? Is this our longest game yet?"

The irrepressible glee of a poker player on a good run is a surefire annoyance to everyone else at the table—and Eddie was bursting with it. Despite the late hour, he looked fresh and neat. If not for the flecks of gray in his black hair, he could have passed for 10 or 15 years younger.

"Rules are rules," sighed Frank. "It's winner-take-all."

Though Frank and James were years younger than Eddie, the hours of play seemed to have strained them more. Both had dark circles under their eyes and were chatting less and less. Frank's mid-cheek sideburns were looking less manicured against his five o'clock shadow, and James's sandy hair was looking greasy and deflated.

"Glad my wife's not here. She'd have all the cash earmarked already," Eddie said.

"Does she know you've been working on your game?" Frank said. "You seem to be at a whole 'nother level compared to last time we played."

"Aw shucks," said Eddie. "Maybe I've practiced a little. I've also had a lot of luck. You're aware how important luck is, right, Frank?"

"Hey Lee, don't we get a snack if we're still playing at this hour?" James said, yawning.

"Chef's working on it," piped up Angela. "Should be ready any minute. It'll be a treat."

Lee Glastonbury pulled Angela aside. "It's what we discussed, correct? With the first box of ingredients we provided?"

"Absolutely. Nothing's changed since you asked us to get started 30 minutes ago, Mrs. Glastonbury," Angela said. "Please don't worry, Chef Ming understands the dietary issues and promised to use only your ingredients. I'm sure everyone will love what he's preparing. He's got a special touch with pastry. Did I mention he trained at Le Cordon Bleu? He brings both an Asian and a continental flair to everything he makes. He's a genius!"

Angela was aglow with pride about the chef. Her hiring coup had caused quite a buzz in local hospitality circles. She hadn't shared it yet with Bea, but she secretly looked forward to him one day turning the inn into a culinary sensation.

Moments later, the ballroom doors opened, and two servers wheeled in carts with aromatic coffee and mouthwatering, just-fried doughnuts.

"World's healthiest doughnuts—and the most delectable," the server said, bringing small plates with two pastries each to the players. "The twisty golden brown one is a French cruller, and the darker one is Belgian chocolate. I've just tried one myself, and I can assure you that you won't miss those unhealthy ingredients."

Eddie Kawai held his plate to his nose and inhaled, looking delighted. "Just the energy I'll need to finish off my opponents. They smell fantastic. You're sure they're gluten- and nut-free?"

"Absolutely," said the servers.

James and Frank grabbed plates and dug right into the luscious, cakey delights. "My compliments to the chef," said Frank after a big first bite and a big swig of coffee. "Don't count that prize money just yet, Eddie. I'm re-energized."

"Don't you worry," said Eddie. "I'm more than up for a challenge."

Once everyone in the room was enjoying their doughnuts, the second server offered each guest a French press with their choice of exotic coffees from Hawaii or Guatemala. Injected with caffeine and sugar, the room buzzed again. The side game livened up again.

"Maybe I will sit in on that cash game," Bea said. "Those doughnuts are like rocket fuel! That chef of yours is great, Angie—congratulations to you."

But Angela had already turned away from Bea and was walking across the room toward the tournament table. She was staring at Eddie Kawai.

His cheeks had flushed and his face was starting to swell.

"Oh no," he said, fear washing over his face. "I need... the shot. I'll be OK, I'm sure I'll be OK."

A hush fell over the room as people began to notice Eddie's distress. The tournament dealer looked at Perry, who signaled to pause the game. Eddie reached into the inside pocket of his tuxedo and pulled out a pen-like injector. With shaky hands, he removed the cap.

Still watching him intently, Angela cried, "Eddie, no! Not that..."

But it was too late. With a wail, Eddie Kawai dropped the device. He'd been holding it upside down, pressing the wrong end into his thigh. He'd only managed a partial injection into his thumb.

"Eddie, do you have a backup injector?"

Eddie barely nodded no. He'd started wheezing and was wild-eyed with fear.

"Someone call 911 right now!" screamed Angela as she kicked off her high heels and dashed out of the ballroom. Foxy jumped out of his seat and was pulling out his phone. But Aseem was already tapping on his and shouted, "I'm on it!"

Seconds later, Angela ran back into the room, another epinephrine injector in hand. She took off the protective cap and firmly pressed the needle end of the device into Eddie's thigh, releasing adrenaline that could save his life.

"Ambulance on the way," Aseem said.

Eddie was now lying on the floor, with his tie undone and Angela kneeling beside him. Foxy and the twins were hovering near them, looking scared and wondering if there was anything they should do. Perry had his arm around the shoulders of the tournament dealer, who looked white as a sheet. Lee stood expressionless in the corner, away from the fray.

"Please stand back everyone, OK? Need to give him plenty of air. You're looking better now, Eddie," Angela said. "Are you feeling better?" Eddie nodded. "We'll get you to the hospital in no time."

The EMTs arrived and wheeled Eddie out, Angela following alongside the gurney.

"Should we call your wife, Eddie?" yelled Foxy as the gurney rolled away.

"Heck no," joked Eddie gamely, his voice soft and ragged. "I'll be fine. And she doesn't need to know I'm gambling."

As EMTs shut the rear doors of the ambulance, Angela promised Eddie she'd check in with him in the morning. The air was crisp and chilly, and the night was so quiet, the ambulance's siren seemed to pierce her eardrums.

"I'd better go check on Bijou," she told the others as Eddie's ambulance faded into the distance. "All this noise must have woken her."

"Wow, she's something," Foxy said to Aseem as Angela walked away. "So beautiful and smart. Hard to believe she's single. Not for long if I have anything to say about it." Aseem's eyes narrowed, but he didn't respond.

As she walked across the grounds to her suite, Angela felt a sudden exhaustion. The emergency handled, her own adrenaline was crashing. *I wonder how much longer this tournament will last,* she thought, yawning. Bea had told her it still could be a long night, despite the chip lead James now had over Frank.

Behind the door of her suite, Bijou was wide awake and delighted to see her new human friend. She jumped up on Angela's shin, sniffing and barking softly.

"Looks like you could use a quick walk. And some water, too? We'll stop at the kitchen and get a bowl."

Angela clipped Bijou's leash on and the little dog trotted ahead into the dark, starlit grounds of the inn. The pooch sniffed around, exploring her territory and looking for just the right spot.

"All right, puppy, let's get on with it so you can get some rest," Angela laughed.

Once Bijou found her perfect patch, Angela led her back toward the inn entrance. As they approached the door, the little dog cocked her head and let out a low woof of curiosity and suspicion. She tugged at the leash, sensing something stirring out in the night.

"What is it, girl?" Angela laughed. "There's nothing out there."

The dog barked again, louder this time, and grew determined to pull Angela toward the phantom distraction. Angela scooped her up and carried her toward the doors—but then she heard a small engine turn over.

"Was that what you heard, girl? Just a scooter, I think," she said, scratching the dog's tiny head. "Nothing to be afraid of. Some poor person has to go to work before sunrise."

Angela saw a small headlight, then a taillight, disappear into the distance, along with the sound of the motor.

"Let's get you some water." Angela put the dog down and led her into the kitchen to find a bowl. She was surprised to find Lee Glastonbury already there, holding the handle of a wok with an air of suspicion. In her other hand was a large, half-empty bottle of a golden oil.

"Mrs. Glastonbury—what are you doing back here?"

"Angela, I think you're the one who should be answering questions. For starters, I thought you told me the chef would use only the ingredients we provided."

"Yes, that's true. Why do you ask?"

"This wok appears to have a residue of peanut oil," Mrs. Glastonbury said, bending down to sniff the pan. "This must be the oil he used for the doughnuts—that's what poisoned Eddie. Here, you smell it. Be careful—it's still warm."

Angela took a whiff from the pan and recoiled. It smelled like peanuts.

"The chef used this oil for the doughnuts, and he should have recognized it would poison Eddie."

Mrs. Glastonbury held the bottle up to show Angela the label: Grade A Refined Peanut Oil.

"I'll speak to the chef in the morning," Angela stammered. "I'm sure there's an explanation. Even if it was the peanut oil, it was an accident."

"A perfectly avoidable, potentially deadly accident. We provided all the ingredients specifically to prevent this," Mrs. Glastonbury said curtly.

"Let's just hope Eddie's all right—for all of our sakes."

Angela nodded soberly.

"I'm heading back to the ballroom," the client said. "Can I assume you'll join me?"

"Yes. I'll be there shortly." Water bowl in hand, Angela hurried out to put Bijou in her suite for the night.

"WHAT HAPPENED?" Angela said quietly to Bea.

Bea and Angela were standing in the corner of the ballroom. Perry, Aseem, and the dealers were closing up the tables. They'd exchanged the cash-game players' chips for currency and were securing the chips for storage in the safe. The tournament had wrapped a while ago—just minutes after Eddie's ambulance left for the hospital.

"Something I never thought I'd see in my lifetime," Bea said. "Frank forfeited."

"I guess a lot can happen in the time it takes to walk a dog. Do you mean he let James win? What's the big deal?"

"$100,000—he just walked away from $100,000—that's the big deal."

"Oh right, I get it—winner takes all. Did he say

why? Could he have felt sure he would lose, anyway?"

"He said that they were both tired, and he was so short on chips he probably wouldn't win—which is true. But every tournament poker player knows you always have a chance to come back and win, even when the odds are long. Every poker player knows that all you need to win is a chip and a chair."

"Guess these rich guys truly don't care about the money," Angela said.

"I've never met anyone rich enough not to care about $100,000."

"I haven't, either," Angela said. "Plus, Mrs. Glastonbury said they were all about the competitive fire."

"Exactly. Forfeiting is hardly the mark of a true competitor," agreed Bea. "Some players at the cash table looked downright shocked—like your new admirer Foxypants. The twins looked pretty confused, too."

"Sorry to interrupt," said Aseem, "but Perry and I are done here. I just wanted to say I still haven't got your fingerprint loaded into the locks on the control room and safe, Angela. Can we take care of it now?"

"Sure—if it won't take long. I'm wiped out. Are you, Perry, and Bea already set up to access it?"

"Yes—you'll be the fourth and last person. I promise it won't take long." He was looking at Angela as if he hoped it might take a while, but she didn't seem to notice.

"Well let's do it, then. Best be sure we're all able to get in… just in case." She paused, wondering if she should tell Bea about the confrontation she'd had with their client in the kitchen. Better to deal with it after a night's sleep, she decided. They'd both be thinking more clearly after a rest. Besides, what could be done about it at this hour? "So Bea, I guess I'll see you in the morning? I've got news, too, but it can wait until then."

"OK, you crazy kids stay out of trouble," Bea said, winking in her usual hammy way. Angela responded with her usual eye-roll. "Perry? Ready to go?"

"Hey, you crazy kids stay out of trouble, too!" Angela said brightly. But Bea and Perry had already left the room.

CHAPTER 9

"Wow, hoodie and gloves? Must be cold out there," Eddie said in a low voice to his visitor.

In front of the sink in the tiny bathroom, Eddie was doing his best to freshen up with a prison-quality hospital toiletry kit. He'd changed out of his hospital gown into his tuxedo pants and t-shirt. The gown, his shirt, and the jacket were draped on the bed frame. He'd unplugged his monitors to prevent their annoying beeping—and to avoid alerting any medical staff that he'd disconnected himself.

"Thank you so much for coming so quickly, at such an early hour. I'd imagine the game went quite late."

"No worries. As long as I get four or five hours sleep, I'm fine. I was only dozing when your text arrived," replied the visitor, who'd taken a seat in the worn guest chair, making note of Eddie's cell on the table next to it.

"Do me a favor, keep your voice down," said Eddie. "They wanted me here 24 hours for observation, but I feel fine. If one of the nurses hears us, they'll put me back in that bed!"

"I don't think we'll have any trouble sneaking out of here. There's hardly anyone working in this dinky hospital. The one nurse at the desk looked half asleep. She didn't even notice me."

"It's a real country outfit," Eddie chuckled quietly. "Closest to the inn, I guess, but not what you call state-of-the-art. Had to press the call button five times just to get a pitcher of water."

"Oh yes, that reminds me, I brought what you asked for," the visitor said, pulling two jumbo smoothies out of the paper bag he brought with him. The visitor placed them on the table by Eddie's phone. "Got to the juice shop right as they opened. Sounded so tasty, I got myself one, too."

The smoothies looked pink and cold and delicious, with little beads of condensation clinging to the sides of the plastic cups. The visitor took two straws out of the bag and popped them into the cup lids.

"Thanks. Can't wait for a taste. I'm so thirsty and hungry, it will hit the spot," Eddie said, still at the mirror, running a cheap gray comb through his hair. "So, did James win last night's tournament?"

"Yes," said the visitor, omitting the unusual detail about the forfeit.

"I thought I was finally going to win one," said Eddie genially, "I mean, don't get me wrong, I haven't forgotten I said there was something rigged about the game, but that was just a weak moment. I get a little emotional sometimes. Please don't tell anyone. And don't think I'm going to flip out like that nutjob Billy Ray or anything. I have no intention of spoiling our vibe like he does.

"But I sure would like to win one," Eddie paused and chuckled. "It's not like I can't afford to lose. We can all afford it, right? It would just be fun to win. That's why I've been practicing so much. Even got a poker coach."

"I heard you'd done that—Bill Malmuth, right? The ten-time World Series bracelet winner?"

"Yeah, well my big goal is the Main Event of the World Series. This tourney's just for fun and good practice."

"We've all noticed how much your game's improved. You're kind of outclassing the field now," the visitor said, with a knowing chuckle.

"I don't know about that," laughed Eddie. "But I've been working on it. Anyway, you still need a little luck in tournament play, right? In the past few years, haven't some of us been getting all the bad luck and some all the good? Don't think either of the twins have won, have they? Oh, there was that other guy who took one down a few years back—then had that massive heart attack. That was sad. Since he croaked at the hospital, he didn't even get his winnings—what with the rules about being present at the award ceremony and all. I guess that's what you'd call a cooler, huh?"

"That's running bad for sure."

"So I guess the extra money—it goes to the charity, right?"

The visitor didn't respond. Eddie emerged from the bathroom and put on his tuxedo shirt. "None of us players are too interested in the charity, if we're honest," Eddie said, laughing again. "Just a good excuse for a big-money game."

The visitor nodded and smiled.

"Thanks again for coming. You were the third person I tried. No surprise that everyone else was asleep at this hour. I would have had to call a rideshare, but I don't know if they would have picked up that smoothie for me," Eddie laughed.

The visitor grinned and picked up the two smoothies, passing one to Eddie. "Cheers," Eddie said, smiling. He took a long draft of the thick, sweet concoction. The visitor took one, too.

"Delicious, isn't it?" said the visitor.

"Nectar of the gods. Reminds me I'm glad I'm not allergic to fruit," Eddie laughed. "If only raspberries had caffeine, I'd be ready to jump back into the tournament. I know we won't start again until tonight, but can you tell I'm dying to get back to playing poker?"

But almost as soon as he said it, Eddie realized something was happening to him. Something bad. Something all-too-recently familiar. He sat down on the bed to steady himself, his face crumpling with fear and sadness.

"'*Dying to play poker....*' That was perhaps not the luckiest choice of words," said the visitor dispassionately. Eddie had started to sweat, his face flushed.

"Could I have given you my smoothie by mistake? You reminded me you can't have nuts, so absolutely no almond milk. The one with almond milk was supposed to be for me."

The visitor picked up both cups and looked at

the paper labels clinging to their sides. "Oh dear. Mine says no almond milk. That means yours... oopsy."

Eddie's face swelled even faster than it had the night before. His throat closing, he was straining to breathe.

"Don't you worry, Eddie," the visitor said calmly, standing up and moving toward him. "I'll get you some help. I'll get that one tired warhorse of a nurse. But first, lie back on the bed. Let's loosen your collar. There, now let me just adjust this pillow to help with your breathing."

The visitor pulled one of the pillows out from under Eddie's neck. Eddie laboriously lifted his head so that the visitor could replace the pillow behind it. The corners of his mouth turned up a little, hope flickering in his panicked eyes.

"There, there, just lean back," the visitor said. "I'll get the nurse soon. But first, let's take care of that noisy wheezing. Remember, you said you didn't want anyone to hear us."

Eddie's breathing was tortured, his eyes once more shining with terror. He saw the pillow coming towards his face and tried to scream, but only managed to croak out "help" so faintly that the visitor almost couldn't hear it.

The visitor pressed on the pillow. It didn't take

long. It required almost no force at all. Just enough to muffle Eddie's feeble cries and amplify the anaphylaxis. Within a moment, Eddie lay still.

"There, that's better," whispered the visitor, placing the pillow back under Eddie's lifeless head. "Bye, Eddie."

Hoodie zipped to the top, the visitor pulled the laces, drawing the cap in tight. With gloved hands, the visitor picked up the two smoothies and the paper bag and grabbed Eddie's cell phone off the table. Then the visitor slipped out of the room, walked unnoticed to the back stairwell, and trotted out of the hospital.

CHAPTER 10

Earlier than she might have liked, Angela awoke to the unfamiliar sensation of her cheek being caressed by wet sandpaper.

"Well, that's a new experience. Good morning to you, too, Bijou," she laughed. "Are you trying to tell me something? Let me put on some clothes and we'll have another walk."

After dressing herself presentably in record time ("I can't just throw on sweats, puppy. We've got guests"), Angela clicked Bijou's leash onto her collar and the two of them headed out the door.

Out on the grounds, Bijou decided upon a spot near the one she and Angela had visited before. Afterwards, Angela tried to lead her back into the inn—but the dog pulled on the leash, just as she had the night before.

"You want to poke around a little?" Angela said. "I suppose we can take a few extra minutes." Bijou pulled Angela along toward the big empty barn that stood in the fields behind the inn.

"Not much to see over here, girl." The barn's old-fashioned red paint was peeling in places, and some of its planks appeared to be breaking down. "Bea and I haven't figured out what to do with this old thing."

The dog continued sniffing and pulling on her leash until they reached the overgrown grasses and gravel behind the big old structure. Bijou's tail wagged when she found an unexpected treasure: a fast-food wrapper with a hamburger remnant inside. Someone had dropped it beside the barn.

"That's what you're all excited about? Don't eat it, girl," Angela said, pulling the paper away from the pooch. "We'll find Connie and get you a better breakfast."

Strange, thought Angela. The wrapper and the remains of the burger looked fresh. She also noticed an old wooden ladder that had been on the ground had been moved and turned upright. It now reached up toward the second-story doors of the hayloft at the back of the barn.

Curious, she decided to slide one of the big barn doors open. It stuck so hard, it took three big tugs before she was able to move it and step inside the dilapidated building.

"Anticlimactic, don't you think, girl? Unless you like cobwebs and rusty farm implements."

The barn's interior had the same abandoned appearance Angela remembered from when she and Bea first checked it out weeks ago. *Maybe Bijou's trying to tell me we need to fix this big shack up,* Angela smiled to herself. *No argument from me.*

"OK, let's go, short stuff." Angela leaned against the door and pushed hard to slide it back into place. "Phew. Let's go find Connie and get you your breakfast."

Connie answered the door of her suite in a bathrobe. Without makeup, in the mid-morning light, she looked tired and tense. *And there's something else in her eyes,* thought Angela—*Connie looks a little sad.*

"Come in for a minute," Connie whispered. "Billy Ray's in the shower."

Angela sat down in an armchair by the window, facing Connie, who sat with Bijou on the unmade bed.

"He must have an awful hangover."

"He doesn't get hangovers, not really," Connie

replied, her speech colored with her subtle Southern drawl. "Professional-grade drinking skills."

Angela could think of nothing to say, so she just smiled sympathetically at Connie.

"I've always wondered if he married me for my inheritance or the endless supply of his favorite whiskey. Smart money's likely on both."

"Why did you marry him?"

"I didn't want to be alone. And he was nicer back then. He thought I was pretty—and least I thought he thought that."

Angela opened her mouth to speak, but once more was at a loss for words. She decided to change the subject.

"Bijou and I had fun. But I think she's hungry now, so I thought I should bring her back."

"Do you think you could take her again tonight?" Connie said brightly. "It's just—I think she stresses him out when he's playing poker. He so wants to win."

"Sure, I'll take her again. Just be careful, I'm getting attached to her," Angela said, reaching over to scratch the dog's little head. "You said Billy Ray really wants to win. Do you think he was serious about thinking Mrs. Glastonbury picks favorites somehow?"

"I don't know. I mean, he started complaining about that at the last two events. But he always wants to play again."

Angela felt her phone vibrate and pulled it from her pocket: a text from Jackson at the front desk.

`Urgent phone call for u, Ms. Garcia. Offered to take message. Says he needs to hold.`

"I've got to go. Don't forget, we've got coffee and muffins and other things to eat down in the breakfast room. Maybe I'll see you there later."

"Thanks."

Angela gave the pup one last pet before heading out the door. "See you later, sweet girl."

"THAT WAS AN INTERESTING NIGHT," Bea said. "Ready to compare notes?"

Bea and Perry were sitting at one of four round tables in the inn's breakfast room. Sunlight was streaming in through a large window. They each had in front of them a pastry and coffee, chosen from a buffet on a sideboard against the wall.

"Yes," Perry agreed. "Now's our chance to discuss the tournament while your opponents aren't here. Or Lady Lee."

"The players might be sleeping in. Lee may be afraid her flesh will burn in direct sunlight," cackled Bea. "What do we make of her special tournament?"

"Where to start?" said Perry. "Let's see, how about her strange rule about all three of your buy-ins staying in the prize pool, even if you have to leave? And that no prizes will be awarded until breakfast after the last game?"

"Seems like the rest of us players got a very lucky break when Eddie got sick. I keep thinking maybe a player slipped him a peanut. If someone did, do you think they realized Eddie could have died?"

"I was wondering about that," said Perry. "Angela saved the day—and Eddie's life. You're right that even though it didn't kill him, we'll likely have one less player competing for the $100K tonight. And the odds improved for Frank and James when he left last night—since Eddie was by far the chip leader."

"Someone could have been hoping for that

exact scenario. Less competition, but no blood on the hands, either," Bea said. "Speaking of 'competing,' what did you make of Frank forfeiting last night?"

"He just walked away from $100,000! You don't see that every day," Perry said, laughing out loud. "It doesn't seem like something you do if you want to get rich. Or stay rich."

"Something else I noticed—I'm not sure, but I think the chip stacks might have been altered after Eddie went to the hospital. Like Frank had even fewer chips than before, and James's stack had somehow grown."

"I thought some chips had been moved during one of the breaks," Perry said. "But I wasn't sure. We could watch for it tonight—and check the video later."

"Were Frank and James also playing a lot of hands together? Seemed like an odd coincidence. And did you also notice both of them raising a lot at the start of the hand, with one of them always abandoning ship without even seeing the flop?"

"You thinking it could be some kind of collusion? As in, one of them helps goad a third player into building a pot for their buddy?"

"Something like that."

"It fits. I'll ask Aseem to show me the video before we start again tonight."

"Good morning, ladies and germs," said Pat, bounding into the room. She was wearing a soft, plaid flannel shirt and baggy jeans.

"I've got big news," said Pat, helping herself to coffee and a muffin. "Mind if I sit down?"

"We can't say no after that intro, can we?" snarked Bea. "Spill it, sister!"

"I started looking into the reviews this morning, Bea—and I found something interesting."

"I knew it! They *are* all written by the same person."

"I think so. But there's bigger news than that." Pat leaned forward toward Bea and Perry and whispered. "We should keep it to ourselves for now, because Angela's not going to like it."

"What won't I like?" Angela said, arriving at the wrong moment. She looked quite serious—even more so than usual. "You might as well tell me, because whatever it is, I guarantee it is not the worst news of the day. Go on."

Bea nodded at Pat, encouraging her to continue. "Well… I shouldn't have, but I looked into those negative reviews. Before you get mad, I looked at them on my own. Bea didn't help me. I just got curious."

Angela raised an eyebrow at Bea. "Yes, yes, I'm quite convinced that Bea wasn't involved, and there was no plan to respond in any way."

"It's true, Angie! I've been busy with poker," Bea said. This was, strictly speaking, true—Bea had been busy playing and helping Perry with poker. But it was hardly sincere. Bea would have happily joined Pat in her detecting if she'd had the time. And Pat was only digging into the reviews because Bea asked her to.

"What else? Might as well tell me everything."

Cautiously, Pat continued. "Somebody's started a blog, and it's all negative comments about Betty and the inn. I think it's the same person who's been trashing Betty's book. There's a new review on Betty's product page. And—shock of the century—it links to the blog."

"Big deal," Angela said. "That's all you got?"

"You're taking this awfully well. I suppose your rule about not responding goes for the inn, too?" Pat said. "I mean… not that we were planning anything."

"We've got much bigger problems than bad reviews. My news is dreadful," Angela said, sighing sadly.

"You mean like the fact that our secret event is not so secret anymore?" barked Billy Ray, storming in. He was holding up a tablet computer and pointing at an article with a large, grainy picture of several of the players arriving at the inn. "Not quite the complete privacy Lee promised."

Angela took the tablet from Billy Ray with one hand and covered her mouth with the other. "How on earth? No one could have known we were even open." Color drained from her face as she tried to puzzle out how anyone could have found out about the secret event.

"Angela, you OK?" said Foxy. He'd just entered the breakfast room with Rex and Max, all three of them looking freshly showered. The twins wore preppy slacks and sweaters. Along with his designer jeans, Foxy wore a fitted t-shirt and cardigan emblazoned with the logo of his fancy car.

Foxy hurried to Angela's side. He wrapped his arm around her shoulders protectively.

"Would you look at that?" he said, pointing at the picture on the tablet. "Isn't that Walter and Harry arriving—and James and Frank right behind them? OK if I take a closer look?" He tapped the screen of the tablet and scrolled down. Under the picture was a block of text with a huge headline in an ugly font:

"The Truth about Betty: The Queen of Christmas Just Wants More Money!!!"

The sloppily written paragraph was chock-full of texting shortcuts and misspellings, but still managed to drive home its mean message.

Foxy pulled a cell phone in a gaudy gold case out of his pocket. "What's that web address? I'll snap a pic if no one minds—I might like to check it out myself later."

Angela shook her head in disbelief. "We're not even officially open yet, and we're getting slammed."

"Didn't you say a bad review was no big deal?" Pat said.

"It's the pictures. Someone's trespassing and spying on our event." Angela scrolled down and found another grainy evening shot of Mrs. Glastonbury speaking with Frank and James in the driveway, all of them dressed in their evening finery.

"I'm sure we'll get to the bottom of it," Angela stammered, composing herself. "We'll have someone walk the grounds during our event tonight. We'll shut the drapes of the ballroom, so no one can see in."

"And block the beautiful moonlight?" said

Connie Bandy, who'd followed her husband in and now stood passively behind him, Bijou at her feet.

"You'll still see the moon through the transom windows. But because they're high up, above those huge doors, no one will be able to see in from the outside."

Lee marched into the room, Walter and Harry just behind her. She was back in her old-money-matron tweed garb. "I guess you're thinking better late than never works for security, Angela?"

"Nice that you're blaming everything on Angela, Lee," said Foxy, moving between Angela and Mrs. Glastonbury. "Didn't you promise us you were personally overseeing the security?"

"Last time I checked, Drew, Angela was running this establishment. Or not running it, as the case may be."

"I was already wondering why I keep coming back for these shindigs, Lee," brayed Billy Ray. "Am I the only one who notices the same people always seem to win? And I ain't one of 'em. Now we can't even count on privacy. What, exactly, is in it for us players? The coffee's nice and all, but I can get one of these muffins down the street for five bucks. If Connie and I wear shades, there's a good chance we can do it without seeing our picture on some sleazy website."

Angela winced. "Lee—er, Mrs. Glastonbury—why don't you and I step outside to talk? I'm sure we can figure out who took this photo, and I promise we'll tighten up the security tonight. Everyone else, please sit down and enjoy your breakfast."

Angela wiped a tiny bead of sweat from her brow. The atmosphere in the room was becoming stuffy and warm. The tension seemed to add a few degrees to the temperature.

"Before we go outside, wasn't there something else you wanted to tell everyone, Angela? I am well aware you've heard the important news of the day. Would you prefer I tell them?" Lee said sourly.

"I was about to tell them when you walked in." Angela paused and exhaled audibly. "I'm sad to have to tell you… Eddie has died. I heard from the hospital a few minutes ago. The coroner is investigating."

Silence fell over the room for a moment, except for Connie's gasp. The others looked stunned.

"Coroner… does that mean they think it's… murder?" blurted one of the twins.

"Well, ain't that grand?" said Billy Ray. "Now we got a murderer in our midst! And here I was thinking a dirty game and a sleazy reporter were the worst things I had to worry about. Watch your backs, people."

"No one's said anything about murder. The hospital said that it's standard practice to investigate when someone dies in a hospital under irregular circumstances," said Angela. "But the police do not suspect foul play. Eddie was trying to leave against medical advice, and no one noticed, so no one could stop him. Then they think he had another reaction—something called a biphasic reaction, meaning it was related to the one he had last night. In all likelihood, it was a tragic accident."

"That doesn't mean no one was at fault, Angela," said Lee sternly.

"Mrs. Glastonbury, why don't we find a private place to talk?"

"Sure, how about the kitchen? I'd like to make sure your chef is not destroying any evidence."

"Everyone, please enjoy your breakfast. I'm very sorry for the inconvenience, but I promise Mrs. Glastonbury and I will work out the security issues. Also, although this is not a murder investigation, the police have asked that no one leave town for the next couple of days. Please don't worry, it's only a formality. Of course, with two more nights of tournaments to go, I can't imagine any of you were thinking of leaving. But I promised to pass that information on to you.

"Now Mrs. Glastonbury, shall we?" Angela said, motioning toward the door.

"Angie, hold up," said Bea. "I'll join you if you don't mind."

She hopped down from her seat behind the large table. "Nice outfit," Perry leaned over and whispered, grinning. Bea winked at him. "Festive, no? Too bad I forgot my elf hat."

Bea was wearing red and green striped harem pants with a crotch that sagged to her knees, paired with her standard sheepskin boots. On top, she wore a holiday sweatshirt boldly decorated with sequins, a large image of chocolate blocks, and the message, "I FUDGING LOVE CHRISTMAS!" in huge letters.

"Um, Bea, perhaps you'd like to change first?" said Angela, taking in the full measure of Bea's appearance with a familiar sense of futility. Lee stared at Bea with disgust.

"They're dance pants. What's wrong with dance pants?" Bea said. "I admit, it might not be elegant like the outfits from our gift shop, Angie.

But you can't say it's not merry. We don't have to be elegant when we're not playing poker, right?"

With a forced grin plastered on her face, Angela leaned in to speak directly into Bea's ear. "Bea, you must realize that's not the kind of outfit Mrs. Glastonbury would approve of. Why don't you put on a pretty sweater from our shop? And some plain black pants?"

"Is it possible you're taking kowtowing to your client a little too far, Angie?" Bea whispered back. "I'll do it—for you, Angie. Don't start that meeting without me."

"Mrs. Glastonbury, let's meet in the kitchen, as you suggested, in half an hour. OK?" Angela said. "In the meantime, please enjoy some coffee and a pastry."

"Provided it doesn't poison any of us," Lee said. "I'll see you in the kitchen in 30 minutes. Don't be late."

CHAPTER 11

"Bea, wait up," said Pat, following Bea out into the hall. "Can we have a quick chat while you change?"

"Good idea."

Back at their suites, the adjoining doors between them were open, allowing them to talk while Bea changed in privacy in her own room.

"So where the heck did you even get that outfit, Bea?" Pat laughed. "It doesn't look like something Angela would pick for the Betty Snickerdoodle line."

"I ordered it from Rebecca—the internet tube," Bea said. "It's like magic. All the rooms have one—do you see yours in the corner? I use it for everything: shopping, research, my alarm clock. I even use it as a phone. Once the inn's officially open, we'll use it for room service. You say 'Rebecca' to wake her, then say what you want. You could use it for your detecting, too."

"Us detectives tend to shy away from those devices for research. I don't believe they have an incognito mode. Good first lesson for you: private detecting's about finding tracks, not leaving them."

"Incognito mode—I like the sound of that. It sounds like real detective talk."

"That'll be our first lesson: basics of web research. OK for me to come in now?"

"Yes," said Bea glumly. "I'm changed."

Pat entered the room and began to laugh. Just giggles at first, then full-throated guffawing.

"What's so funny? This is a 100% Angela-approved holiday ensemble."

Bea was wearing a black cardigan with a frilly collar that went up to her chin. It had a prim white bow around the neck and tiny holly decorations embroidered at the wrists. As Angela suggested, she wore black pants with it. The only part of the outfit that looked truly Bea was the footwear: black Velcro-strapped sneakers.

"This sweater's going to sell for $180 in the gift

shop. It's already selling like gangbusters on our website."

"I'm sorry, it's hard picturing you as a schoolmarm," Pat giggled. "What will you wear tomorrow? A habit?"

"It looks very chic in the catalog. At least that's what Angie tells me. Besides, Betty's fans are very modest. They like things sweet."

"You ain't joking that you and Betty are two different people."

Bea scrunched her eyes to figure out how to respond to Pat's comment. Did she not realize that Betty wasn't a person at all? People were so illogical!

She decided to change the subject. "My meeting's in a few minutes. Any progress on Operation Troll Patrol?"

"Yes. That blog with the pictures and the nasty article about the inn could be a big clue. It's hard to get anywhere with anonymous reviews on an online store. But his website and domain give me more to go on. I'm working on it."

"Still thinking they're the same person?"

"Pretty sure. Plus—here's the best part—it looks like they used a cell phone to snap those pictures. That may help me figure out more later. Sometimes there is metadata stored with photos."

"Don't forget, you have to show me how you're doing all this stuff. I want to catch the review troll as quickly as we can, but I also need to learn how to be a detective."

"I know, I know. We'll have a lesson once I learn more. I was wondering if you wanted me to check into any of the poker players. This situation with Eddie's death, Billy Ray saying the game's rigged—does it seem a little fishy to you?"

"More than a little. Perry and I are keeping an eye on the play. Maybe you should check into any connections between the players. And check into Lee's background."

"I'll do some digging about the charity, too."

"Then don't forget—we have to compare notes. And you have to teach me how you found everything."

"I got it. Oh, and I've got a connection at that hospital. I'll see what else I can find out about Eddie's death."

"Oh boy, we might get lucky and have a real-life murder on our hands!" Bea said, rather gleefully. "That didn't sound right. You know what I mean."

"Dude's dead either way. No chance of hurting his feelings."

"Good point!" said Bea, holding her hand up for a high five.

~

BEA ARRIVED in the kitchen and found Angela already there, pacing the floor.

"Girlie, you gotta calm down. Just because Madame Bossybritches complains doesn't mean you did anything wrong. Some people are always unhappy. She seems like someone who gets her way all the time by being impossible to please."

"I want so much to impress her," Angela said. "Imagine the referrals we could get if we pulled off an exclusive event like this! But now I'm impressing her with how bad things are going. I hope we can do damage control. A client like her could make our reputation or break it."

"One client can't make or break our entire reputation, Angie. Besides, are you sure we'd want a steady stream of picky richies coming through the inn? People like Lee Glastonbury, who are never satisfied with anything? Are you forgetting the inn was supposed to be a place for Betty's fans?"

Angela stopped pacing and looked at Bea. "You're right. It wouldn't hurt to be able to do the occasional posh event, though, would it? Especially if we can bring in this kind of money. More than that, I wanted to do this right. To prove that I can."

"You are a perfectionist, no doubt about it."

"Thank you for changing your outfit."

"It's not exactly my style. But at least it's still pretty comfortable."

"Bea, there's one other thing I'm stressed out about. And I don't know if we can fix it. Mrs. Glastonbury told me last night she thinks Chef Ming made a mistake that caused Eddie's reaction —which means she thinks he killed Eddie."

"What?!" said Bea. "That's just—"

"Ladies," said Mrs. Glastonbury, striding into the kitchen, "let's not waste time. First, about those infuriating, unacceptable photos, do you have any idea who on your team leaked? And, pray tell, what you plan to do about it?"

"Why do you assume it wasn't one of your entourage, Lee?" Bea said.

Lee glared at Bea.

"Don't worry, Mrs. Glastonbury," Angela piped up. "We'll remind everyone that this event is private."

"It's a little late for that," sneered the client.

"And we will have someone sweep the grounds for trespassers. Aseem, Pat, and I will start tonight, taking turns walking the area. Those photos will be the last."

"We're trying to track the owner of that blog down, too," said Bea. "We'll send a strongly worded letter about removing those photos once we do."

Angela waited a beat for Mrs. Glastonbury to turn away then mouthed "Really?" in Bea's direction, smiling. Bea responded with a wink and a nod.

"That would certainly be an improvement. Now about the death of Eddie Kawai," Mrs. Glastonbury continued. "This is a matter much less easily resolved. Angela, how do you plan to respond?"

"What do you mean?"

"I've already shown you the evidence that your chef caused the allergy attack—the peanut oil in the wok. That means the inn must take action. I'd like you to make a clear show of responsibility. And I'd like the chef replaced for the safety of my guests. I'm making no promises, but this might be a way for you to avoid legal action."

"But Mrs. Glastonbury, I'd like to at least talk to Chef Ming first. He'll be here any minute, and we can sort out what happened."

"Besides, now that Eddie's gone, so's our allergy

problem, right?" Bea interjected. Angela put her hand on her forehead, looking like she might faint. "Just saying, Angie. Why should we fire Chef Ming when there's not even any reason to anymore?"

"I'm not saying you have to fire him, Angela," snapped Mrs. Glastonbury, "although I can't imagine why you wouldn't. It's your reputation. You do what you have to do. What I'm saying is I want a public acknowledgment of responsibility. And I don't want that chef in the kitchen for the remainder of our event. I trust you will comply with this request."

Her directive delivered, Lee marched out of the kitchen. As she whipped through the swinging doors that led back into the breakfast room, she crashed right into Foxy—who'd been crouching behind the door, eavesdropping. The collision knocked him to the floor. Mrs. Glastonbury peered down on him, momentarily dazed.

"Well if it isn't Mr. Foxy!" Bea said. "Perhaps your new nickname should be Snoopy. Can we help you with something, Snoopy? Snacks in the breakfast room not to your liking?"

Ever smooth, even in disarray, Foxy picked himself up off the floor and instantly recomposed himself. "Not snooping. I thought Angela might need a little moral support. Angela, I just want you to know, I think you're doing a great job. And I think the other players agree."

Angela beamed and coyly tilted her head. "It's nice to be appreciated, Foxy."

Mrs. Glastonbury rolled her eyes. "Mr. Foxworth, I am quite sure you don't speak for our entire group. And in any case, the success of our event is my responsibility. I kindly request you stay out of these affairs."

She turned on her heel, fuming, and headed out of the kitchen—keeping her head down to avoid meeting the eyes of the chef, who brushed by her into the kitchen as she was leaving it.

"You wanted to see me, Angela?" said the chef. He was physically trim, his dress tidy. His crisp chef whites were branded with the inn's logo; his head was covered in a tight red bandana. Everything about him radiated a passionate professionalism.

"Yes, I have to share some terrible news, Chef Ming."

"Foxy, I don't think we need you here for this," Bea said diplomatically. "What I mean is, take a hike, Slick."

"She's right, Foxy," Angela said, touching

Foxy's arm. "I appreciate your support, but we need to speak with the chef in private."

"No problem. Perhaps we could meet for coffee or a drink later. I'd just like to check in. And don't forget that tour you promised me."

"I think Angela will be very busy, won't you, Angela?" Bea interrupted. She gave Foxy a little guiding push toward the door.

Foxy complied, but looked back at Angela and mouthed "I'll find you later." He grinned and flashed his mouthful of perfect pearlies her way once more. Bea would have sworn she heard Angela release a tiny sigh.

"How can I help you, Angela?" said the chef.

"There's no easy way to say it," Angela began. She soberly explained that Eddie's allergic reaction appeared to have been caused by the doughnuts, and that, after a secondary reaction, Eddie had died. Haltingly, she then told Chef Ming about Mrs. Glastonbury's discovery of the wok and the peanut oil—which seemed to be the cause of the reaction.

"I get it was an accident, chef. A terrible, innocent mistake. But surely you can understand that Mrs. Glastonbury has reason for concern. She'd like you to step aside for the rest of the event."

"No, I don't understand at all," the chef replied

firmly. "There's no way I caused that poor man's death."

"The wok's still on the stove, and so's the peanut oil," Angela said.

"I didn't put them there. How would I have produced all those doughnuts using a single wok? What a ridiculous idea. I used the brand-new deep fryers, and I filled them with palm oil—as anyone who knows how to fry doughnuts would. You can even see doughnut sediment in the tray."

Angela and Bea leaned in to see the minuscule traces of fried dough that had dropped into the tray.

"Of course, there's not much. The fryers hadn't been used before."

"But chef, that still doesn't explain the peanut oil—there's residue in the wok," Angela said.

"I don't need to explain that," said Chef Ming. "I have no reason to lie. No chef in his right mind would use a wok to prepare doughnuts for 20 people. More important, I am a trained professional and would never put an allergic guest at risk."

The chef dragged two boxes out of the walk-in refrigerator. One was clearly labeled "Donut Fry Oil. 50 lbs." "It's solid palm oil. And as you can see, it's mostly empty. The fryer takes 40 lbs."

Angela and Bea watched as the chef picked up each item from the second box.

"These are the ingredients we used to make the doughnuts—all provided by Mrs. Glastonbury except the fry oil."

The chef held up a canister with a handwritten label: "gluten-free flour," followed by vanilla bean paste, imported French baking chocolate, organic eggs, local butter, and empty envelopes labeled "organic yeast."

"I even saved the empty bags and bottles," said the chef. "I didn't want there to be any doubt I'd used all the ingredients."

"Thank you, chef," said Bea. "Mrs. Glastonbury must be mistaken."

"Even if she is mistaken, she is our client," said Angela. "Chef Ming, I'm sorry, but I have to ask you to sit out the next few days. I'm sure you understand. Customer's always right and all that."

"No, I don't understand," replied the chef, his face flush with emotion. "This is beyond ridiculous. Beyond insulting. I'm meticulous about food safety—and about guest satisfaction. Isn't that why you hired me? If you can't trust me, there's no point in having a relationship at all. I have a reputation outside your inn to maintain, too. I hardly intend to make this the last stop of my career."

The chef yanked open the snaps of his chef's coat and tossed it onto the shiny stainless steel chef's table.

"Good luck, Angela. For tonight, check the second box in the walk-in. I've already done most of the prep for dinner. You'll just have to find someone to cook it—I mean, if you can trust I didn't poison the food when prepping it. For tomorrow night—and the rest of your life—you're on your own."

"Chef, there's no need to be so hasty," Angela said, taken aback by the chef's angry reaction. "I don't want to lose you. She's just a very important client. I thought you'd understand."

"Sometimes you have to choose, Angela. I can't stay where I'm not trusted. I realize you're new to this, but I thought you would have more backbone." He spun around and stormed out of the kitchen.

Angela looked stricken. The chef's assessment of her maturity hit a nerve.

Bea looked at Angela with slightly raised eyebrows. "You sure this is how you want to play it, Angie?"

"Bea, why can't you see we need to please her?"

"Girlie, I don't like your chances of pleasing her, no matter what you do. Bullies like her aren't ever satisfied. Was it worth losing Chef Ming over? You worked so hard to lure him here. He's gonna have another job in a heartbeat."

"It's still possible he used that peanut oil," Angela said weakly. "Technically, we can't say for sure he didn't cause Eddie's death."

Almost on cue, Chef Ming opened the door a crack and spoke through it.

"If you're still thinking I might have killed Eddie, better think again. Even if I'd used the peanut oil—*and I did not!*—read the label. It's *refined* peanut oil. No peanut solids. The odds of it causing a reaction are practically non-existent. Kind of like your reasons for getting rid of me. If you want to run a hospitality business, get a clue!"

"Chef Ming, please wait—" Angela said. But he was gone before she said it and not looking back.

"What now, Angie?" Bea asked. But Angela was in no mood to talk, her self-induced stress reaching a new peak.

"Please save it, Bea. I'll figure something out," she replied, rushing out of the kitchen.

Bea inspected the half-empty peanut oil on the stove. Chef Ming was right: the label said it was "highly refined." A box of plastic gloves sat behind it on a shelf. She pulled one onto her right hand, carefully picked up the oil, and carried it with her out the door.

~

FOXY WAS EAVESDROPPING AGAIN, more carefully this time. He chided himself about his earlier carelessness: Unacceptable. A rookie mistake.

He was standing near the break room doors when he heard Chef Ming exit out the back of the kitchen, toward the parking lot. Time to hustle!

He jogged down the inn's hallways, scanning for anyone who might see him. He had to be sure the other players (or, heaven forbid, Lee) didn't notice what he was up to. Finally Foxy spotted Chef Ming standing by his car on the far side of the lot.

"Chef, wait up," he said, taking a deep breath as he walked across the lot, reestablishing his air of cool self-assurance. "I overheard what happened. I'm sorry."

"Yeah, I'm not used to getting accused of poisoning people with my food. Especially when there's plenty of proof I didn't do it. But whatevs. Angela's got some learning to do. Some growing up, too."

"What if I told you," Foxy said, looking around to be sure he wasn't seen, "that I'm looking into what happened to Eddie—quietly. Would you be willing to help? The thing is, we'd have to keep it between us."

"Why not? You're a rich dude, right? Will you think of me for your next fancy dinner?"

"Sure," said Foxy. "You'll be the first person I think of when planning my next soiree." Foxy reached into his pocket for his wallet. "Remember," he said, finger to lips, "hush-hush."

The chef made a zipper motion across his lips. Then he hopped into his car and drove off.

Foxy turned back toward the inn and scanned the scene once more. No one else was in the parking lot. But was someone standing at that window? Foxy thought he saw a drape drop back into place. He decided it must have been a shadow.

BEA ARRIVED BACK at her suite and realized she'd somehow misplaced her card key. *Drat,* she thought. She didn't want to tromp all the way to the front desk carrying the heavy, slippery bottle of oil one-handed—especially since she wasn't sure anyone would even be there to help her. She might drop it on the way, or have to tote it all the way back to her suite if no one was working the desk.

Bea put the oil down next to the door of her suite, intending to leave it there while fetching a new key. But what if someone saw it and wondered what it was doing there? What if someone saw an opportunity to destroy evidence?

She picked up the bottle and knocked on the suite next door to hers: Pat's.

"Can I use your internet speaker to call the front desk? I lost my key."

"Come in," said Pat. "You don't even need to call for a key. You can go through the connecting door to your suite. I don't think you locked your side."

"I guess I figured if yours was locked, we'd be good," replied Bea, setting the bottle down on the desk.

"Interesting thinking from someone who had a manuscript stolen not that long ago. Better start thinking like a crook if you want to learn to be a detective."

"I might have if I'd thought a crook had moved in next door!" Bea said defensively. But inside, she was a little annoyed with herself. She was an expert at sniffing out shenanigans at the poker table. Those were the same skills she needed to transfer to her detective training—the things that would bring her whodunit yarns to life—yet here she was, acting all trusting.

"What's with the peanut oil—and the glove?" Pat said, opening the connecting door to Bea's suite.

"Hold your horses, I'll tell you in a minute," Bea said as she walked back into her suite. She used the internet speaker to call the front desk and asked them to bring her a new card, then rejoined Pat and plopped onto the bed.

"Well, if you don't want to tell me about your mysterious bottle, I've got a few tidbits to share," Pat said, scrolling through notes on her laptop. "Shall I start with Operation Troll Patrol? I got lucky and found metadata on the review bomber's photos—including the name of a professional photographer in San Francisco. That's the good news."

"Show me," said Bea. Pat gave Bea a quick demo of the software she used to analyze digital photos. "Wahoo! I'm starting to feel like a real detective now. Does this mean we're homing in on our culprit?"

"That's the bad news. I called the photographer. He hasn't owned the phone for a while. He sold it to one of the pawn shops he uses to buy camera equipment. Doesn't remember which shop.

"I'm gonna call the pawn shops he mentioned. But it's a longshot. Pawn shops sell tons of phones. Unlikely they'll know who they sold it to. Even if they do, they might decide the information's private. The phone's really old—that might narrow it down at least. But we have to assume the photos might be a dead end.

"I'm still working one other lead," Pat continued. "The website where the pictures were posted. The domain is masked—but sometimes you can get the host to cough up the owner if you pay a little money. I might be able to track down our Betty hater that way. You cool with covering that expense?"

"Heck yeah," said Bea. She grinned as she imagined a cloak-and-dagger deal with some nefarious character—a real noir scenario. "Long as we do that together."

"The IP address of the blog appears to be in San Francisco—like the pawn shops. Not much to go on. If we can get the registration data, that will give us a starting point. We'll have a little hope, anyway."

"We can do it. Jessica Fletcher solves crimes with a lot less."

"Would you give it a rest with the Jessica Fletcher?" Pat grumbled. "If this were *Murder She Wrote,* the culprit would simply incriminate themselves and Jessica would just happen to be the only person there to hear it! Detecting isn't like that in real life."

"Sheesh. No need to get so oversensitive."

"Sorry. It's just if I had a dime for every time a client expected me to work miracles like a TV sleuth... well, let's say I wouldn't be working here with you. If we were on TV, the review bomber would helpfully drop his phone right in our laps," Pat said, getting worked up again.

"We don't technically know it's a 'he,'" said Bea.

"Ugh!"

"No need to be sexist."

A knock on the door of Bea's suite provided a welcome interruption. Jackson had come by with Bea's new card key.

"Thank you, Jackson. Sorry for the trouble. And listen—could we keep this between the two of us? I know it's a lot of work to keep creating these cards, and Angela will worry it's bad for security—"

"It's no trouble at all," Jackson said. "There is a

risk of someone finding your card and using it. But the system can tell us if anyone entered your room using the lost one. And we can easily make you a new card and deactivate the old one."

Bea thanked Jackson again and shut the door behind him. His comment about the card key system gave her an idea. She called Aseem and asked him to come help her and Pat with a little tech project—and to bring his laptop.

"So how about our other mystery?" Bea said as she walked back into Pat's suite. "Any luck finding connections and dirt on our suspicious poker people?"

"Not yet. I haven't gotten too far. I started looking into links between the players. There doesn't seem to be anything at all on the internet about Walter Wells, real estate developer. If I hadn't seen him with my own eyes, I'd say he doesn't exist."

"Lee did call him 'reclusive,'" Bea said.

"True. I'll keep digging on that, and the other players. But I also started looking into Mrs. Glastonbury's children's charity—another complete mystery."

"Why am I not surprised?" said Bea, chuckling. "I'll try to remember to ask her tonight. Could it be registered under a different name?"

"Possible," said Pat. "But it's not the first possibility that leaps to my mind. What's up with the peanut oil? Since you wore a glove, I assume we won't be popping corn later."

"How are you with fingerprints?"

"Not great. Like I told you, private detecting's not like you see on TV. Most of my work is done right here," Pat said, pointing to her computer screen.

"I get it. No fingerprint analysis. I was planning to start with internet research, anyway. First thing I wanted to find out is whether peanut oil is the same as peanuts when it comes to allergic reactions. I was also wondering where you can buy this brand. Is that something we could find out? It looks like it's packaged just for restaurants."

"You are starting to sound like a detective. Those are all questions we can dig up answers to. Why peanut oil? And what's so special about this particular bottle?"

"Maybe it's nothing. But I think somebody might be using it to make it appear our chef caused Eddie's death. Lee found the oil, and she says it caused the reaction. But the chef says in no uncertain terms that he didn't use the oil. He even quit over it."

"Huh. If everyone's assuming the death is an

accident anyway, why would someone need to make sure it looked like the chef's fault?" Pat said. "What if it wasn't an accident—but pinning it on the chef was meant to make it seem like one?"

"Chef says he not only didn't use peanut oil, it can't even trigger an allergic reaction."

"If he's right, we can catch a killer in a good old-fashioned frame-up!" Even Pat was getting excited about the prospect of a murder case. It would be a heck of a lot more interesting than digging up divorce dirt.

"It's great, isn't it?" Bea said. "I don't want to get my hopes up, but it's looking more and more like we're in the middle of a real-life murder mystery."

"That reminds me, I spoke with my hospital friend. She said while it's likely Eddie just had a secondary reaction—a repeat of the first attack, like they told Angela—it's possible he was exposed to another allergen at the hospital. That's why the doctor's interested in the autopsy."

"That fits with what I was thinking," said Bea. "What if someone triggered a new reaction on purpose—because the first one didn't finish the job? They might try to cover their tracks by making it look like it was the chef's fault.

"Perry and I figure all the poker players could

be suspects. They all benefit from Eddie's death—one less competitor for the big money."

"Even if they eliminate a player," said Pat, "they still have to beat everyone else to win the money. That makes the game seem like a pretty weak motive for murder."

"I agree. If players are secretly teaming up, though, the motive's clearer. Take Frank forfeiting to James last night—it seemed plain weird, but it's not if they're splitting their winnings. If they're splitting their winnings, they only have to make sure one of them wins."

"Aren't these guys all mega-rich? Are they going to kill someone for a hundred grand?"

"Good point, that part doesn't fit. There must be more to the story. There's plenty of other weird behavior. Like Foxy—he's been nosing around in everyone's business. I wonder what that's about."

"If anyone, I'm wondering about Lee," Pat said. "Since she's the one who found the oil."

"The silent but deadly theory?" Bea said.

"As in, 'the one who smelt it dealt it,'" Pat said. "It's a multi-purpose rule. And an important concept in detecting."

"But the 'he who denied it, supplied it' corollary points the finger back at the chef," Bea said.

"Lee seems more likely to have a motive. What happens if a player can't claim their winnings? Could be her charity gets a big windfall donation," Pat said. "I wonder if that's ever happened. Could be another piece of the puzzle, and I bet there are more."

A knock at Bea's door interrupted them. Pat popped her head out of hers and greeted Aseem and invited him in.

"So Aseem," Bea said, "Can you keep a secret? A big one. You have to keep it even from Angela."

Bea explained how she and Pat came to believe that one of the poker guests might have exposed Eddie to peanuts on purpose—perhaps going to the hospital before dawn to finish the job—and whoever it was might now be trying to pin the crime on Chef Ming. Could the card key system track the guests' comings and goings? Could the system say whether anyone left in the wee hours and returned to their rooms later that morning—sometime after Eddie died?

"Angela would not approve," Bea said. "She wouldn't like us spying on guests, and even though we're trying to catch a killer, the possibility of a crime would freak her out—so mum's the word."

Aseem nodded. He opened his laptop on Pat's

desk and logged onto the server. “The system only tracks when keys are used,” he said. “It can tell us when people enter their rooms, but not when they leave. But it’s a start.”

The room access log showed that from an hour after the tournament ended until just before ten o’clock in the morning, none of the guests entered their rooms.

“Only Angela used her room key during that period—that must have been after she took Bijou for a walk.”

Bea raised an eyebrow.

“I’m staying out in the casitas, right on their path. At one point, I heard the dog barking.”

“Don’t worry, I don’t think you’re stalking her,” said Bea. “Even if maybe she’d like you to.”

Aseem opened his mouth to respond, but seemed to think better of it.

“I’ll mind my business,” said Bea. “Back to the matter at hand. Does this mean we’re at a dead end? It’s possible some guests left their rooms, am I right? But, if so, none of them reentered during the night. Which means it’s likely our guests were all tucked in their beds—does that sound right, Aseem?”

“That’s what it looks like.”

“Fudge!” said Bea. “Thank you anyway,

though." Before shutting the door behind him, she reminded him not to tell Angela she and Pat were nosing about the guests' comings and goings—or that they had suspected one of the guests might even be a murderer.

"It was less than eight hours between the end of the tournament and everyone showing up at breakfast, so I suppose they could have been innocently sleeping," Bea grumbled.

"Don't forget Eddie might have died of a secondary reaction caused by the exposure he had in the ballroom—and that exposure might have been done on purpose by someone here. Nobody would've had to go to the hospital to finish Eddie off," Pat said. "Say someone dosed his doughnuts. Maybe that someone didn't want Eddie dead, but wanted him out of the tournament. Or they wanted to scare him. And now Eddie's died from a secondary reaction, and that someone realizes they're an accidental murderer, and they're desperately trying to frame the chef with that oil bottle."

"What Ming said about refined oil is key," said Bea.

The two women huddled behind Pat's laptop, searching for proof of what the chef had said about peanut oil and allergies.

"Well would ya look at that?" said Pat. "Chef Ming was right—doctors say highly refined peanut oil is fine for most people with peanut allergy. It might not completely clear the chef—but it's looking much more likely that Eddie was exposed some other way."

"I wonder if Ming even bought that oil," said Bea. "If we can figure out where it came from, and who bought it, we'd have our framer—and our killer. That's a project for later, though. We're running out of time to get ready for tonight's festivities."

Bea walked through the adjoining door back into her suite—then let out a squeal of delight.

"Hot diggity!" she said, pausing dramatically in the frame of the connecting door. "I figured out how a killer could go to the hospital and come back without being tracked."

"I get it," said Pat, noting Bea's dramatic pause between their rooms. "Brilliant! The killer could have left their room and come back in through the suite next door without a key, as long as someone was there to let them in. Now we just have to see who's rooming next to whom."

"Let's hurry up and get dressed. If we're quick, maybe you can find out what suppliers sell that peanut oil and I can figure out whose suites are connected before we head down to the event."

"Sounds like a plan. Congratulations—we've got the beginning of a theory."

"Is it too early to start calling me J.B. Fletcher Junior?" cackled Bea.

CHAPTER 12

As he left Pat's suite and headed to the ballroom, Aseem considered Bea's joke about Angela. Though he didn't know her well, Bea had never struck him as the matchmaking type. She'd always been the cranky hermit who somehow became Angela's favorite client. He'd always figured Angela's affection for Bea was mostly about the work. There was nothing that motivated Angela more than proving herself, and Betty's books had provided plenty of opportunity to show what an incredible marketing whiz she was.

But in the months since that insane episode with Cash, the bond between Angela and Bea seemed clearer. And was it his imagination, or had

Bea's sharp edges softened a little? She'd shown a lot of gratitude for Angela's help in building her book empire. Creating and running the new inn, and building a media business around it, was a huge opportunity, one he knew Angela was thrilled to pursue. Bea was investing in Angela's future, and entrusting Angela with her own future, too.

He couldn't have been happier for Angela. Her energy and her vision were infectious. And he had a valuable role of his own to play in Betty Snickerdoodle, Inc., too, bringing smart tech solutions to their media enterprise. He laughed to himself, thinking maybe *this* was the big startup opportunity he'd always hoped for. OK, so it wasn't in Silicon Valley, but he could be part of something that would one day be huge.

Now that's a cruel irony, he thought. If he'd known helping Angela with a startup would be a possibility, he'd never have fallen for Cash's get-rich-quick sales pitch. But then, if he hadn't fallen for Cash's stupid plan, maybe the inn wouldn't be happening, either. The chain reaction that made the Betty Snickerdoodle brand bigger than ever was kicked off by Cash's failed plot to steal Bea's work.

Cold comfort, though. Remembering how he'd

swallowed Cash's nonsense didn't exactly make him feel like a genius—and it was hard to imagine it had made him look good in Angela's eyes, either.

Before Cash, his relationship with Angela—his girl Angel—seemed to be moving in a different direction. Like, out of the friend zone after all these years. That seemed out of the question now.

Back in the day, before Bea and Betty consumed most of Angela's time, they'd teamed up on all sorts of small business projects. They'd even developed a little following because of their ingenious solutions for cash-strapped small businesses. She'd bring her talents for marketing on a shoestring, and he'd supply clever tech solutions. Now, though, as he neared the ballroom, he wondered if Angela even remembered that resourceful Aseem.

Helping Cash—however innocently—could hardly have made him seem like boyfriend material in Angela's eyes. But even more than that, Aseem realized with a sigh, if he worked in Angela's company, she'd be his boss. And everybody knows getting involved with the boss is a very bad idea. He had to believe Angela would never make that sort of risky mistake.

"There you are," said Perry, interrupting Aseem's thoughts. "I'm dying to see that video."

"Sorry, got waylaid by Bea. I hope you haven't been waiting long."

"Not long. Can we get started, though?"

"Of course. Shall I open it, or would you like to do the honors?"

Perry nodded and touched the fingertip sensor on the control room door. "Thanks. I get a little kick out of that."

"State-of-the-art technology magic," laughed Aseem.

Once inside, Aseem sat down in front of the server and entered his password. "It'll take a second to start up the software. Then we'll check the video it stored last night."

The software's interface appeared. Aseem clicked a few keys and opened some files. "Give me a minute."

After a few more clicks, his expression grew gloomy. "Let me check in another spot," he said quietly. Finally, after more clicking and searching, he turned to Perry.

"I don't know what happened. No recording was saved. I'm sure I checked everything, and the test recordings from the two nights before the event started are here and they're fine."

"Did someone tamper with it?"

"That's my question, too."

Aseem checked the Wi-Fi connection first. "Wireless looks fine." He got up from his chair and checked the cables in and out of the server—they looked fine, too.

He stepped out of the control room to inspect the camera installed above it. "Everything's still connected."

"I'm… I'm baffled. And I'm sorry. I'll test it again now and reset everything for tonight. I'll check some user groups to see if anyone else has had a problem."

"Could we set up an extra system?" Perry said.

"Like a redundant system? Good idea," said Aseem. "I'll check into it. I think there's enough time to install one by tonight."

"Sounds like a plan," Perry said, leaving the control room and heading out of the ballroom.

Nuts, thought Aseem. *So much for restoring my image of indispensable brilliance!*

CHAPTER 13

Foxy stopped at the front desk on his way back to his suite. "Can you tell me which room is Ms. Garcia's?"

"I'm sure you understand, Mr. Foxworth, we don't give out suite numbers without permission. Do you mind if I call her first?" said Jackson.

"Of course. And nice work, Jackson," Foxy replied. "I mean, as a guest I appreciate your concern for security."

Permission granted, a few minutes later Foxy was at Angela's door. She looked anxious, but brightened as soon as he grinned and trained his gleaming chompers in her direction.

"Come in. Can't chat for long, though. I'm

trying to figure out how to avert the next few disasters."

"Chef Ming?" said Foxy. "I heard."

"You heard? I can't believe the word is already traveling around the inn!"

"Oh, well, I just happened to run into the chef —I don't think anyone else knows yet," Foxy fibbed. "I won't tell anyone, I promise."

Angela sat down on the edge of her bed. "It doesn't matter now. Everyone will know when there's no dinner in a few hours," she said, tears welling up. She brushed them away and cast down her eyes. "Some company president I'm turning out to be!"

"Now, now—don't overreact," Foxy said, sitting down next to her. He put his arm around her shoulders and gave her a reassuring squeeze, then gently lifted up her chin. "Why don't you tell me what happened?"

"I'm not sure I should. I mean, it's a personnel matter. Shouldn't I keep those things confidential? You're a guest here, for heaven's sake. See what I mean? I don't even know what I'm doing."

"Don't I seem trustworthy to you?" Foxy beamed at her again, his snowy teeth illuminated by some magical internal moonlight, the tiny crinkles around his eyes seeming to whisper "trust me."

Angela hesitated a minute. "Well—you might be able to help."

She explained that Mrs. Glastonbury had requested—insisted, really—that the chef not prepare any more of the food for the event, since she assumed he caused Eddie's reaction. Mrs. Glastonbury had even produced evidence—a half-empty bottle of peanut oil. But Angela admitted she wasn't sure if it was even evidence at all.

"Lee is a piece of work!" Foxy said, leaning in to hear more.

"It's not all her fault. Maybe I should have pushed back. It didn't occur to me that the chef would quit over it. Really, I just didn't think at all," Angela cried, head in her hands. "Because who will prepare the fancy food you people expect, now that we have no chef?"

Foxy was stumped. What the heck did he know about high-brow catering? He was determined to help, though. He knew that if he came up with something, anything, she'd go for it—not just because he was overwhelming her with his potent charms (if he dared say so himself), but because she took for granted his insider knowledge about the food preferences of the filthy rich.

"Please don't worry, Angela. We'll figure something out," Foxy said. "How about this. Why not mix it up a little? Nobody likes fancy food all the time. There's a place near here that's famous for gourmet hamburgers. I went to a wedding once where that restaurant served miniature versions. They had the waiters bring them on silver trays with white gloves, as if they were caviar. Everyone loved it!"

"Do you think that would work?" Angela said.

"I don't see why not. I could call them—drop the name of the bride and groom, see if they could do a rush job."

"We'll pay extra for the rush," Angela said, perking up a little.

"Hey, how about this? We add a little music to the cocktail hour—to match the more casual vibe."

"An ironic chic type of thing?"

"Haha. Well, if you have to give it a name," Foxy said. "I've got a great playlist we can download. Maybe that tech guy of yours—Akeem, is that his name?—can set it up to play in the ballroom?"

"Aseem? Yes, good idea. I'm sure he can help."

Foxy thought he noticed a little pang of emotion flash on Angela's face as she mentioned Aseem. Guilt?

"See? It's all coming together," said Foxy. "Let's get started."

Foxy called the gourmet burger joint. Given the ridiculously short notice, it took some persuading, but when he dropped the names of the bride and groom he knew—VIPs, it seemed—the restaurant said they'd make it work.

Then Angela came up with a clever idea of her own: she called her mom, Maria, for help with the third night's dinner.

"It's... it's... well, it's an emergency. And I promise, it won't be too hard, Mamá. Chef Ming prepped everything for tonight, but we've found a restaurant to help cater tonight—so we'll hold the prepped ingredients for tomorrow. All you'd need to do is cook, and add your toque de amor, Mamá —your touch of love. Muchas gracias, Mamá! Te quiero!"

"She said she'd do it," Angela told Foxy, grinning from ear to ear. "I say a few words in Spanish and she's powerless to refuse almost any request."

"Like a superpower," Foxy laughed.

"Oh, it is," Angela said. "Especially given how many talents she has that I can tap into. Of course, I am smart enough not to abuse it. My kindergarten-level Spanish also keeps me in line."

Angela stood up and faced the door. "I'm so

sorry, Foxy, but I've only got an hour to get ready for tonight. OK if I see you later?"

Foxy stood in front of her and looked into her eyes with his mesmerizing gaze. "You look so beautiful already. How long can it take to change into a dress?"

"Oh, there's more to it than that," Angela laughed. Then she took a deep breath. "Foxy, I don't know what I'd have done without you." She beamed and threw her arms around his neck to give him an exuberant hug. But as she did, she felt cold, hard metal bump against her hip.

"Foxy… are you wearing a gun?" she said, stepping back.

Crap! thought Foxy. *I didn't see that hug coming. Man, I am off my game today. It's like I'm starring in an episode of amateur hour.*

"You can't be too careful in my position," Foxy said, placing his hands on Angela's elbows and looking into her eyes. "A close friend of mine was carjacked—the thieves got away with his Ferrari and about a thousand bucks. With all the cash we had to bring here, I just thought… I'm so sorry if I scared you, Angela. Don't worry, it's licensed, and it's got a safety."

"Sure, it's OK," said Angela. But looking at her,

Foxy wondered if the spell he'd been casting was coming undone.

CHAPTER 14

Mrs. Glastonbury was evidently not pleased. She'd cornered Angela near the ballroom doors to deliver a sotto voce tirade. In the center of the room, servers circled with elegant trays of sliders and crystal parfait glasses filled with adult milkshakes. The guests were gobbling them up with delight.

"Hamburgers? You're serving *hamburgers,* Angela?"

Good grief! Angela thought. Getting any sort of dinner together on such short notice was a magic trick. The guests were having a fabulous time. With the heavy drapes closed, the room was darker than the night before—but no worries about trespassers getting a peek at their party.

And Foxy's music—a blend of pop favorites and carols—contributed to a happy vibe in the room.

"Technically, they're not *hamburgers,* Mrs. Glastonbury," Angela said sweetly. "They're sliders."

"I expected something upscale."

"But they are upscale—very upscale. They're Wagyu beef. I can assure you they're quite delicious—but you don't have to take my word for it. Why don't you try one? I could make a plate for you."

The client looked as if she'd rather die. "No, thank you."

Bea and Pat stood a few feet from Angela's semi-public reprimand, Pat guarding the ballroom's center door. Bea elbowed her in the ribs.

"I guess it only makes sense she won't eat a hamburger, since she's such a cow!" Bea snickered. "The milkshakes supplied by her relatives must be off-limits, too."

Angela shot Bea a glare. Bea cackled louder. Angela sighed and gave up. Catering to Lee Glastonbury's insatiable demands was getting more than a little old.

"Mrs. Glastonbury, this was a quick solution for tonight. You realize we no longer have a chef. The good news is that tomorrow we'll prepare a delicious dinner from the ingredients you supplied. Tonight's caterer was recommended by one of your players, Mr. Foxworth. Was I wrong to think he'd be a good judge of what his fellow players might like?"

"Angela, may I speak with you?" said Bea. "Lee, you don't mind if I steal her away for a moment, do you?"

Lee glared at Bea and walked to the other side of the ballroom where Walter and Harry were standing, enjoying their shakes.

"Bea, I'm pretty sure she heard that 'cow' comment," Angela giggled. "I shouldn't laugh, but, honestly, I'm over some of her pickiness."

"About time! I wanted to tell you good job on getting the dinner together."

"I couldn't have done it without Foxy."

"That's nice. Still not sure I trust him. He's after something from you."

"You don't trust anyone," Angela said reflexively, even though Foxy's gun—and what it might mean he was up to—popped into her head. "Don't worry, I'm keeping my eyes open."

"By the way, you look beautiful. I don't think Foxy and I are the only ones noticing." Bea tilted her head toward Aseem, who was standing near the control room, eyes glued on Angela.

"You're imagining things again, Bea." But as she said it, Angela checked that the hem of her sweetly sexy gold dress was straight, and touched the back of her updo to make sure all was still in place. She looked over at her old friend and smiled, then moved next to Lee for her announcement.

"Uh-huh," laughed Bea.

Lee tapped on a glass with a knife. "It's time to begin our second poker tournament. Aseem, could you please turn the music off?" Aseem switched off the music and restored the crackling Yule log video to the ballroom's big monitor.

Billy Ray Bandy was by the bar. He'd grabbed the bottle of Heavenly Mash from the bartender's hand and was topping off his half-empty shake with whiskey, splashing some over the side of the glass. "Any reason we can't have music while we play, Lee?" Foxy raised his milkshake as if toasting in Billy Ray's direction.

"In the past, we've kept our games quiet to allow better concentration. There's a lot of money at stake. But if no one objects, we could play the music at a soft volume."

"Don't turn off that Yule log, though," Billy Ray said. "Can't have too much holiday cheer.

Speaking of which, what do you think of my belt buckle, Sexy?"

He'd opened his jacket and was leering in Angela's direction, tilting his crotch forward to display a large metal Western belt buckle with a green and red painting of mistletoe on it. Underneath the design, "KISS ME UNDER THE MISTLETOE" was printed in huge letters.

Standing right at his side, Connie had a close-up view of her boorish husband's performance. Her face looked hot with humiliation.

"Check it out—it's got mistletoe painted right on it. Get it? Festive, huh?"

Angela felt like she wanted to vomit at the implications. Though she'd asked for none of Billy Ray's crude attention, she felt guilty for what Connie must be feeling. She noticed the twins putting their arms around their dates protectively. Foxy moved to her side to do the same to her, but Angela deftly dodged him and stepped forward. Aseem looked at her, distressed. She collected herself and mouthed "It's OK" in his direction.

"Mrs. Glastonbury, please continue—are we ready to begin? Aseem, let's leave the music off for now. Why don't you head outside for a sweep of the grounds? Pat just got back. You take this turn.

I'll take over after you. Mrs. Glastonbury—over to you."

Mrs. Glastonbury seemed relieved for the assist, and she looked at Angela with approval for the first time in two days.

"Yes, let's get started, shall we?" Mrs. Glastonbury said. "Ready, Perry?"

Perry nodded.

"Does anyone need a reminder of our rules?" The room was silent. "Good. Then Perry, please shuffle up and deal."

The players looked for the seat cards with their names on them and arranged themselves at the tournament table. Bea plopped down in seat seven, with Foxy on her left in seat eight and James in seat six. Billy Ray was at the opposite end of the oblong table, standing unsteadily beside seat two.

"It's lucky that you and that belt buckle of yours are way down the other end, Billy Ray," cackled Bea. "I doubt I'd be able to control myself! I'm a strict observer of mistletoe etiquette.

"Good luck, boys. Thought I should warn you, I'm gonna try harder tonight! I've been reading poker books all afternoon. I'm ready to try out everything I've learned."

"Don't forget, to win, you've got to play well

and run well," said Foxy. "Run well as in get a little luck on your side. You feel lucky, Bea?"

"Pretty lucky. Maybe not as lucky as you, Foxtrot."

"They say it's better to be lucky than good," said James, exchanging smirky grins with Frank and Harry. They were settling into their seats, along with Walter, Rex, and Max.

"Amen to that," said Bea.

"If it wasn't for bad luck," Billy Ray said, careening into his seat, "I'd have no luck at all."

"I don't think that's true, Billy Ray," snorted Bea. "You've made it this far."

WITHIN A FEW HOURS, Foxy, the twins, Harry, and James were out of the tournament. Foxy and the twins were waiting for another player or two to bust out, so they could restart the cash game at the second table.

Billy Ray, Walter, Frank, and Bea were still in the tourney. Connie sat behind Billy Ray's seat, looking forlorn. Bijou was sitting on her lap. Billy Ray was running low on chips again. As he had the first night, he was making wild calls and depending on luck to stay in the game. He'd just won another hand, surviving an all-in against Bea.

"See? Seems to me your luck's not so bad," Bea said.

"You're right," Billy Ray slurred. He was even drunker than the night before. "Tonight's my turn to win."

"Ten-minute break, everyone," Perry announced, resetting the clock.

"Billy Ray, honey, I know it's not that late, but I'm tired. I'll drop Bijou off with Angela, then go to bed."

"Oh sure," Billy Ray erupted at his wife. "Why is it whenever I got a chance at winnin', you don't wanna be here?"

Angela moved to Connie's side and took her arm, leading her toward the door. "Billy Ray, the rest of us will watch carefully and tell Connie every detail tomorrow. Shall we, Connie? I'll walk you back to your suite and get Bijou's bowl."

Billy Ray grumbled a little to himself, then made his way to the bar to refresh his drink.

Bea hopped down from her chair and moved next to Frank. "Buy you a drink?" Frank nodded. They walked together to the bar on the far side of the ballroom.

"Frank, seems only right I should inform you, I

think I spotted your tell—actually, Walter seems to have spotted it first. It seems he can tell when you're about to give up. When it's a big pot and you move your hand back towards you and put a chip on the front right corner of it, he comes right after you, and you fold every time. It's like he's spotted a weakness or something."

"Thank you, I guess," stammered Frank.

"I thought you'd want to know. Walter's been getting your number—especially since the stakes have gone up."

"Well, thanks for the drink—better hit the bathroom before we start back up again." Frank strode out through the ballroom doors to the head.

Bea walked back to the empty tournament table, grinning. Perry was standing nearby. "Well, isn't that interesting?" she whispered, tilting her head toward the door. "There goes Walter, hustling out behind Frank—right after I hinted to Frank that I'm on to their racket."

"What did you tell him?" said Perry.

"Just that I noticed when he places his hole cards a certain way, Walter bets him off the hand. I didn't tell him I thought it was collusion, of course. I said I thought he was telegraphing weakness, and Walter was catching on."

"Maybe he realized you were on to them. He also might have believed you were sincere. Most people hustle off to the bathroom during breaks, right?"

"I think he knows I know. And I didn't even tell him I noticed his 'stroke my sideburns' signal."

"One more thing. You looked comfortable at the table a few times tonight. Don't forget your dumb old lady routine."

"Shoot, I sometimes forget when I get tired. Thanks for the reminder. I hope they didn't notice," said Bea, moving back from the table. "I wonder if they're planning to mess with the stacks. Let's move away to give them an opportunity. Take a quick look and remember how much they've got in front of them."

Bea and Perry walked casually toward the patio exit, keeping their backs to the tournament, but sneaking the occasional furtive glance. Bea glimpsed Frank walking by Walter's seat, his jacket pocket seeming to brush against the edge of the table. A couple extra of the highest denomination pink chips had been dropped behind Walter's stacks, where they were slightly hidden.

"Bingo!" she whispered to Perry.

"Aseem tested the video to be sure it would

work tonight. I'll watch it to get the proof once everyone clears out."

"PLAYER IS ALL-IN," said the dealer. Bea was out of the tournament, leaving Walter, Billy Ray, and Frank competing for that game's $100,000 prize. "Flip your cards, please. Let's see 'em."

The two players turned over their hands. Billy Ray's luck had run dry for the night. Walter busted him out with a pair of tens versus Billy Ray's weak suited cards. Walter extended his hand for a sportsmanlike shake. Billy Ray batted it away.

"Screw you," he slurred. "Screw all of you." He pushed himself away from the tournament table, stumbling and almost falling down. Angela looked relieved when Foxy leapt from his seat at the side game and rushed over to help, grabbing Billy Ray by the arm.

"Get off me, Foxy!" Billy Ray shouted, spittle flying. "I can see through your act. Bet you thought your chances would be better tonight, huh?"

"Hey, we both wanted to win, Billy Ray, but that's poker," Foxy said evenly. "Tomorrow's another night. Do you need help back to your suite?"

Aseem and Pat rushed over to Billy Ray's other side to lend a hand.

"Let go of me!" Billy Ray said, cursing. He shook off all three of them, pulled his chair out from the poker table, and wobbled himself into it. "I ain't done talking to you, Foxy. I saw you paying off the chef. A little something for poisoning Eddie, huh? Pretty desperate way to improve your chances."

"What?" sputtered Foxy. "I didn't pay the chef at all—much less for poisoning Eddie. That's just the booze talking, Billy Ray."

"I saw you! From my window. In the parking lot—you pulled something out of your wallet and handed it to the chef. Smooth. Looks like getting rid of Eddie wasn't enough to improve your luck. You gonna kill me next? You've only got one more chance to win. I hope I'm still alive tomorrow to see it."

"Billy Ray, whatever caused Eddie's allergic reaction, it was an accident," said Angela. "And it may not even have been the chef's fault, anyway." Angela looked away as Lee aimed a seething stare in her direction.

"Ha! Then why'dja fire him, sugar britches?" blathered Billy Ray.

"He wasn't fired," Angela said defensively. "I asked him to take a break. He decided to quit."

"Some job you're doing running this place, hot stuff. First, we got a guest getting poisoned, then someone's taking pictures of our 'secret' event." Billy Ray raised his hand sloppily and pointed at Angela, Aseem, and Pat. "Gee, all three of y'all are in here. So who's outside making sure no one's spying on us again?"

"I'm interested in your answer, too," said Lee.

Angela's face burned. "I… I will head out momentarily. I forgot after getting Bijou set up in my room. It's only been a short while. And we've had the drapes shut all night."

"Don't worry, Angie," piped up Bea. "We're almost done for the night." The heads-up play between the two remaining players, Frank and Walter, was winding down fast.

"Then if no one's doing the job, I'll take a look myself." Billy Ray staggered to his feet and headed to the ballroom doors. "I could use a little fresh air." No one in the room could disagree. Pat held the door open for him and gave him a wide berth as he lumbered through it.

"Player all-in," said the dealer. A moment later, Frank was out. Walter was pronounced the winner, and Perry instructed the dealers to close up the games for the night.

Bea and Perry stood beside the table, discreetly comparing notes.

"He technically didn't forfeit tonight, but Frank wasn't exactly fighting to win, either," Bea whispered to Perry.

"My thoughts, too. How tired are you? I'd love to watch the video tonight with you, if you're up for it."

Bea waved Aseem over and asked him if it would be possible to check out the video footage of the night's tournament.

"Sure. I can set it up so you can watch it from your suite."

"Come by in a few minutes. Pat, Perry, and I will be there."

"Should I tell Angela?"

"No, you know how skittish she is. And don't worry," Bea added, seeing how guilty Aseem looked. "We're just checking a few things that could be suspicious, and they'll probably turn out to be nothing. If we see anything important, I'll tell her, I promise."

CHAPTER 15

"Bea, you awake?" Pat was knocking lightly on the adjoining door.

"Huh? I am now," honked Bea. "Where's the fire?"

"Sorry, I didn't mean to wake you. Thought you might be up already. Got some news on our little projects I thought you'd like to hear."

Bea swiveled her skinny little legs off the bed and reluctantly stood up. "OK, I'm up."

"How about I meet you in the breakfast room? Say, in 20 minutes? I could use some coffee."

"Me too. Sounds like a plan."

Bea squinted as she opened the drapes. The sun had been up for over an hour, but it was still early for her taste. On the plus side, getting started early would leave plenty of time for detective play before the game tonight. *Wahoo!*

"Rebecca, play 'Private Eyes.'" A little dancing would get the blood flowing.

After a few minutes of her customary wobbling, Bea felt invigorated. She pulled a cold iced coffee from the mini-fridge and considered her wardrobe options. Both the prim ensemble she'd worn to the meeting in the kitchen yesterday and her "I FUDGING LOVE CHRISTMAS" sweatshirt were lying on the floor. *Both barely worn,* she thought. She picked up the prissy black sweater and shook it. *Looks fine. It's the safer choice, in case I run into Lee or Angela.*

She dressed, brushed her teeth, and splashed a little water on her face. Standing in front of the full-length mirror, she decided she looked pretty good. She didn't notice her tangled bow or the lint and paper flecks stuck to her pant legs. She gave her hair a superficial brush and headed out the door.

Oops. Remembering what Perry told her last night, she nipped back into her suite and grabbed her cane. *That's better. Now I just have to remember to lean on it.*

She shut the door and headed to the breakfast room. Though she assumed no one was watching, she made a big show of leaning on the cane and shuffling down the hall. She was revisiting a technique she'd acquired as a poker player for maintaining a neutral facial expression at the table: Practicing always, even when no one's looking, to ingrain the habit.

Pat had already chosen the breakfast table farthest from the door, in the corner by the window. "Morning, Bea. I got a cup of coffee for you. From the looks of that bow, you can use it." Bea looked confused, so Pat reached over and adjusted it for her.

"Why thank you," said Bea. "What's on your mind? You're raring to go this morning."

"Are you OK? You seemed to be leaning awfully hard on that cane."

"That's great to hear!" In a whisper, Bea explained she was trying to restore her image as a silly and powerless old lady. "What's your big news?"

"It's not all good. Should we start by comparing notes from last night? What did Mrs. G say about her charity?"

"Fooey. I forgot to ask her. She's started giving me the hairy eyeball, anyway. She keeps catching me mocking her. I don't think I'd get a straight answer out of her."

"We can try asking a player about it later. How about I give you my update?"

Pat told Bea she'd heard from her friend at the hospital—and it was looking more like someone had helped Eddie's allergic reaction along.

"They found a trace of a smoothie on his lips, and it looks like it might have contained almond milk—which was as bad for him as peanuts. No one in the hospital would have served it to him. They don't even have almond milk on the premises."

"Do they have any way to track who visited him?"

"Nope. But it must have been before dawn, when only one nurse was on duty. Eddie was found after the morning shift started, during the doctors' rounds."

"Does this mean the cops are hunting for a murderer?"

"Not quite yet. They've still got more tests to do, and i's to dot and t's to cross in the hospital. But my friend thinks it will be soon."

"Helps to have friends on the inside."

"Don't I know it. Half of detecting is on the computer, the other half is friends who can help you out. I've got contacts in the DMV, crime labs, hospitals, hacker networks—anything that might help me track down a bit of dirt. It's all about the network."

"That's not how Jessica Fletcher does it," Bea said.

Pat groaned. "I'm getting a muffin. Want one?"

"Another bit of news," Pat said, firing up her smartphone. She turned it lengthwise, then showed Bea the screen.

"Our troll is back at it!"

"Yep. More pictures and all."

The review bomber's blog had been updated in the middle of the night before. This time, grainy pictures of the poker party in the ballroom were displayed, framed and segmented by window panes.

"Troll must have shot them through the transom windows. That's how they got around the closed drapes," Bea said. "Sneaky! But how did you not see the troll on your security beat?"

"Not sure. I didn't see anyone at all. We could do some poking around the grounds later."

"I wonder if Angela has seen this yet. Or Our Lady Lee the Perpetually Aggrieved. I hope not. I'd like to let Angie down easy."

Almost on cue, Angela walked into the room, Bijou in tow. She looked neatly dressed as always, but tired.

"Morning," she said. "Bijou got me up against my will. I could use some coffee." She draped Bijou's leash over the back of the chair. "Would you watch her for a sec while I grab a cup?"

Large paper cup in hand, Angela returned to the table and grabbed the dog's strap. Bijou was now pulling against it, eager to get outside. "OK, girl, I get it. See you later, ladies. I promised my little friend here a walk, and I've already made her wait too long."

"Angie, mind if I tag along?" said Bea.

Pat hung back in the breakfast room. The baked goods were tasty, the coffee was fresh, and she might even overhear a useful conversation or two, if she kept her nose in her phone and faded into the background.

The players soon trickled in for their morning fuel. James and Frank sat at the table closest to the buffet, farthest from Pat. They looked tidy and serious, Frank's sideburns crisply redefined with a fresh shave, James's sandy hair slicked into place. She could sense them gauging whether she was listening, so she feigned rapt attention to her phone.

One more night, Pat heard one of them say to the other in hushed tones.

What's the plan for getting the hell out of here? came the quiet reply.

Not sure. I hope someone's gonna tell us before the game gets going.

Foxy, Rex and Max, and the twins' twin girlfriends entered the room together, full of high spirits and looking like they'd stepped out of a society magazine. Pat cringed as they grabbed the table next to her, their banter drowning out James and Frank.

"Sorry to interrupt. Mind if we take this chair?" Foxy said.

"Help yourself."

As the five-some downed coffee and the men, at least, chomped on pastries, Foxy led the conversation like a self-appointed master of ceremonies—and a loud one at that. *True to form,* thought Pat. *I don't think I've met a man who seemed more full of himself.*

"Has it been living up to your expectations this year?" he asked Rex—or was it Max? "The tourney, the getaway I mean."

The twins looked at each other. "I suppose so," said one.

"We don't come with 'expectations,'" said the other. "We just like playing a big poker game in a place no one can find us. You get it, right? Once a year, we can get away from investment pitches, sales pitches, piles of legal documents."

Out of the corner of her eye, Pat thought she saw Foxy's head cock at the mention of 'legal documents.' Or maybe it was just her imagination.

The first brother chimed back in. "I bet people who aren't as wealthy as we are think we can do whatever we want, whenever we want," he said. "But we've got a lot of responsibility. You understand what a burden it can be."

Pat accidentally let loose a snort, then tried to cover it with exaggerated coughing. "Pardon me," she said, as the group of five stared. "Coffee down the windpipe."

She walked to the buffet to get a fresh cup and another treat, hoping the quintet would go back to ignoring her. The server had brought out a coffee cake that was fresh out of the oven and releasing a heavenly aroma. She lingered a few moments over selecting a slice, then galumphed as quietly as she could (danged combat boots!) back to her table.

"You know anything about the charity?" Foxy said.

Yes! thought Pat. *Pay dirt.*

"Honestly, not really," said one of the twins, a little sheepishly. "I don't even remember the name of it. Something or other to do with children. We give to so many things, it's hard to keep track."

"The bean-counters add it to the pile for our taxes," the other said. "We more than max out our charity stuff every year. I'm not sure it even matters in the end, but we pass on whatever Lee gives us.

"We're not doing it for charity, even if Lee is," he laughed. "We take her word for it that the charity's doing something good because we want to play."

"I get it. I'm here for the game, too," said Foxy. "Thank you again for getting me in. Now if one of us could win one of these tournaments. One more shot tonight."

"Oh please, Foxy. We took you to the cleaners in the cash game, remember? That's where the real action is."

She might have imagined it, but in a brief glimpse of Foxy, Pat saw a wince. Maybe these stakes weren't peanuts to all the players.

If the players don't even know about this charity how am I going to find anything out? Could government databases, perhaps the IRS, offer a clue? Do public companies have to report their charitable donations? Were any of these rich guys' companies public?

Time for good old-fashioned web research, Pat

thought. She got up from her seat with a groan and decided she'd need more coffee. She was topping her mug off when Connie rushed in, looking disheveled. Her clothes were wrinkled and her hair could have used a brush.

"Pat, I'm so glad I caught you," she said, her voice shaky. "Have you seen Billy Ray? He didn't come back to our suite last night."

I doubt this is the first time Billy Ray's disappeared for the night, thought Pat. *Then again, the humiliation probably doesn't get easier with experience.*

CHAPTER 16

"Aren't you laying it on a little thick with the cane, Bea?" asked Angela as they made their way from the breakfast room to the lobby doors. Bea was staggering like she'd just awakened from a coma and was re-learning how to walk.

Bea put a finger to her lips. "Not so loud, girlie. Perry tells me I've been laying it on too thin. I'm trying to remind people I'm just a clueless old weakling."

"Good luck with that," laughed Angela. "They've already spent two days with you."

Bea hoped Angela was wrong. Her time-tested theory rarely failed her: people were always ready to believe an older person was a nitwit. She had one last night to try to win one of the three tournaments. So far, she'd been putting too much energy into her secret sleuthing and too little into her game. Tonight was her last chance to scoop up a big prize. If she saw someone cheating again, tonight was also her last chance to catch them in the act.

As they made their way onto the inn's grounds, Bijou trotted happily ahead, tail wagging. "Good girl," said Angela, guiding the pup toward the spot she'd favored the night before.

"We got lots to catch up on, girlie," Bea said. "How 'bout I start? Pat and I figured out a few things about our favorite client and our dearly departed chef."

Bea explained that the chef had been right about peanut oil. Even if he had used it—and it seemed unlikely he had—highly refined peanut oil was almost certainly not the cause of Eddie's reaction.

"Lee seemed determined to blame the chef—didn't that seem odd?"

"Maybe she feels guilty," Angela said. "Or wants to be sure no one else is hurt."

"She didn't seem to feel bad about hurting Chef Ming."

"You simply can't imagine she's not a scammer, can you?"

"Seems like she hasn't told anyone very much about this 'charity' of hers," Bea said, making exaggerated air quotes with her free hand.

"OK, OK, I promise I'll ask her about it again, if you promise to give her the benefit of the doubt. Deal?"

"I can live with that. Will you ask her tonight, then? But what about Chef Ming?"

Bijou found a spot to her liking and stopped to make use of it. Then she began sniffing again with extreme determination, pulling Angela along.

"Yes, I'll ask her tonight. And I don't think Mrs. Glastonbury was right to insist we remove the chef, but I can understand her being nervous. We should let it go for now. Just because Mrs. G is demanding doesn't mean she can't also be a decent person—"

Bijou caught the scent of something intriguing. She barked suddenly and gave the leash a sharp tug. Angela was so engrossed in defending her difficult client that the pooch nearly knocked her off balance.

"Bijou!" said Angela. "What is the matter?"

The dog was pulling her back towards the far side of the dilapidated building. "Sorry, Bea, she's obsessed with the back of the barn for some reason. Last night she found a precious treasure—a fast-food wrapper," Angela laughed. "Follow me if you want, or I'll be back in a minute."

The dog tugged more urgently now, and Angela was jogging behind. "My goodness, girl!"

Bea trailed behind. She was keeping up her cautious cane routine, in case someone was watching from their suite. She saw Angela disappear behind the barn a few yards ahead. The little hound began barking excitedly, and she heard her young friend shriek.

"Angie?" Bea said, still a few steps behind.

A moment later, she saw what Angela saw: the crumpled, lifeless body of Billy Ray, lying outside the barn. His neck was twisted. His shoulders rested on a huge boulder embedded in the ground. The loft ladder was lying flat on the grass nearby, a few yards from the barn wall. The barn door was a few inches ajar.

Angela froze in place, her hand covering her mouth. "I didn't bring my phone," she whispered finally.

"Angie, you go back inside and call the police, OK? I'll stay here. Give me the leash. Doggette and I will wait for you."

Angela nodded, regaining her bearings. Bea watched her hurry back toward the inn.

Poor drunken Billy Ray, thought Bea. *Maybe he was right about his luck after all. He sure picked an unfortunate time to try to climb a ladder.*

Bijou was still sniffing and became very interested in something inside the barn. The door's opening was wide enough for the little dachshund, but hardly big enough for a person—even one as slight as Bea.

Bea let go of the leash and the dog trotted inside. Then she hooked the curved end of her cane around the barn door, held on to the straight end, and leaned back with all her might. She pulled and pulled, and the door budged a bit—just enough for her to squeeze through.

"Phew! Now what are you sniffing at, poochie?"

The dog was joyfully investigating a pile of straw or hay at the front end of the barn, just under the loft. Someone had braided a makeshift rope from bailing twine; it was dangling from the loft down toward the straw pile. Whoever made it also left behind a white fast-food bag and a soda cup.

As Bijou inspected the fluffy fodder, Bea got curious, too. She poked around in the pile with her cane, soon hitting something solid. She used the rubber end of her cane to sweep the dried grass away from it.

"Holy mackerel, what do we have here, doggo? Looks like a clue!" Bea bent down and picked up her buried treasure: a smartphone. "Someone's been hiding out here."

Bea didn't know much about cell phones—more accurately, she knew virtually nothing. But she was smart and curious enough to try swiping the lock on the screen. When she did, she saw a photo that looked like one of the ones she saw on the review bomber's blog.

"Dog ziggity, Bijou! It's our troll's phone!"

Bea was so excited, she did a little dance, spinning around with Bijou in a circle in the pile of straw. Remembering that Angela was calling the cops, though, she decided to conceal her exciting find—at least until she could share it with Pat. It would be the perfect bit of evidence for her cell phone 101 training. It might even be the key to solving Operation Troll Patrol!

"Let's keep this clue to ourselves, poochie. I can't wait to show Pat." She felt a slight flash of guilt—what if Billy Ray's death wasn't an accident? And what if the phone's owner had caused it? She shook it off. It seemed obvious that Billy

Ray's drunkenness was what did him in. And if it wasn't, she could always put the phone back in the straw pile where it could be discovered later. She tucked the phone inside her bra and led Bijou back out of the barn.

CHAPTER 17

Angela jogged back toward the barn. She shrugged slightly as she caught a glimpse of Bea's reaction to Foxy, who was running a few yards behind. He arrived just as a local police cruiser crunched onto the gravel driveway.

Surprise, surprise, Foxy inserted himself into the action, thought Bea, eying him.

"Foxy was the first person I saw—he called the police for us," Angela explained. "I asked him to tell the others Billy Ray had an accident. He asked them to stay back until the police could sort things out, didn't you, Foxy?"

"I wanted to help. The twins are spreading the word and keeping everyone calm," said Foxy. "Poor Billy Ray. All that drinking was bound to catch up with him. Look away, Angela. It's very upsetting," he added protectively.

Foxy tried to slide his arm slyly around Angela's shoulders, but she moved outside his reach. Bea grinned at her approvingly. Angela didn't seem to notice, however. She was waving the cop over to the rear of the barn.

"Right here, officer," she called. The coroner's van pulled in behind the cruiser. The cop, a burly man with curly brown hair and a thick moustache who looked to be in his early forties, grabbed a large camera and a big roll of yellow tape from the cruiser and ambled over to the scene.

"It seems rather open and shut, Officer… McGregor," said Foxy officiously, peering at the policeman's nametag. "We all witnessed Mr. Bandy in a state of extreme inebriation last night." Bea watched, fascinated.

"I see. And your name is?" the officer asked. Foxy replied. The officer asked him to step back.

"You must be Miss Garcia," the officer continued, turning to Angela. "Mr. Foxworth mentioned you're in charge here?"

"Yes, I'm the manager here. This is my business partner and the owner of the inn, Bea Sickles. And like Foxy—er, Mr. Foxworth—said, Billy Ray was extremely drunk. We tried to convince him to go to bed, but he refused, and insisted on going for a walk. It's so quiet here at night, we didn't think anything could happen to him. And it was late, so the rest of us were getting ready to turn in ourselves."

Officer McGregor dropped the roll of bright yellow tape on the ground, then began taking pictures and examining the scene. He hung the camera strap over his shoulder and snapped on a pair of gloves.

"No detective, huh?" asked Bea.

"The whole police 'force' in this little town's just a few of us. We multi-task." Officer McGregor squatted down with a grunt next to Billy Ray's body as he spoke. "No signs of a struggle. We'll still have to open a murder investigation, though. We'll need to inform everyone they're not to leave the premises and to be prepared to be interrogated."

"Wait, what?" cried Angela. "But it's so obvious this was an accident!"

McGregor lifted the camera to his face, then shot several pictures of Billy Ray. He looked closely at the ladder's position: it seemed to have dropped directly from the side of the barn, with no added force. He pulled a tape measure from his pocket and took numerous measurements from the ladder to the barn and Billy Ray's body, and took pictures of the ladder from several angles, too. "Sure looks accidental. But for now, anyway, we still have to consider it a suspicious death."

The coroner, a tall, thin, dark-haired man, walked toward the scene, donning his white coat and gloves. Together, McGregor and the coroner examined and documented the scene. The coroner rolled the body over to be sure no signs of foul play were missed. Bea's eyes widened as Billy Ray was moved onto his back, and his jacket fell open. She thought Angela might also have noticed something missing, but her friend's attention was fixed on Officer McGregor's words.

"Any sudden death of a relatively young person is considered suspicious. That goes double for unusual accidents under cover of darkness. And triple for situations where two sudden deaths seem to be connected. Miss Garcia, do I need to remind you about poor Mr. Eddie Kawai?"

Angela opened her mouth to protest, but saw Connie running toward her from the inn, with Pat trailing behind.

"Angela! What's going on?" But from the expression on Connie's face, it was clear she already had an idea what was happening.

"Oh Connie, don't come too close," said Angela, walking toward her. "You shouldn't see this."

It was too late, though. Peering around Angela's shoulders, she saw her husband's body lying still on the ground.

Connie gasped and let out a soft sob, but pulled herself together. "It was bound to happen. Billy Ray was so reckless." A tear dropped down her cheek as she spoke.

"So Mrs. Bandy—am I right that this man was your husband, Billy Ray Bandy?"

Connie nodded.

"And when you last saw him, he was inebriated?"

Connie nodded again, her tears flowing steadily now.

"This appears to be an accidental death. But our protocol calls for a murder investigation. By the way, Miss Garcia, I assume your liquor license is in order?"

Angela blanched and attempted to stutter out an answer. "We're not technically open yet, and I thought since we weren't selling alcohol—"

"Officer McGregor," interrupted Foxy. "May I have a brief word with you, privately?" He wrapped his long arm around the policeman's shoulder. McGregor looked askance at Foxy's inappropriately placed hand. Bea wondered if he was going to smack it off. But the cop allowed himself to be steered away from the scene.

"What the heck is that about?" said Bea, as the four women watched Foxy communicating animatedly with the cop.

"I know. I wish we could hear what they're saying," said Pat.

They watched as Foxy pulled his wallet out of his pocket. With his back to them, he retrieved something from it and handed it to McGregor, but none of them could see what it was. The two men then shook hands warmly. Both were smiling as they walked back toward the barn.

"Foxy here has convinced me we don't need to interrupt your celebration with a murder investigation. We'll let the coroner finish up, and he'll take the body back with him to the morgue to complete his autopsy. Miss Garcia, there is one condition. I still need you to let everyone know they shouldn't leave the premises before noon tomorrow."

"That shouldn't be a problem, officer," Angela said. "Our event runs until then, and I'm sure everyone plans to be here."

"Just make sure of it." He reached into his pocket and offered her and Bea business cards.

"Please don't hesitate to call me if anything arises." He nodded knowingly at Foxy.

"I think I'll head back to my suite now, Angela," Connie said. "Bijou can come with me." Bea passed the leash over to Connie.

"Let me walk you back," said Foxy to Connie, offering his elbow to escort her. *Huh,* Bea thought. He seemed concerned and not on the make—a different Foxy altogether.

"That was weird, to say the least," said Angela as the police cruiser drove away, the coroner's van following behind, carrying Billy Ray's corpse. "It's good that Foxy helped shortcut the investigation, I guess," Angela said. "I mean, I'm sure Mrs. Glastonbury will be none too pleased about any of this, not that that's anything new."

"That Foxy is as smooth as glass and I haven't got a clue what he's up to," said Bea.

"I'm worried about Connie," Angela said. "Maybe I should go check on her. She may need someone to talk to, and Foxy may not be the right person for the job."

"I'm sure you're right about that," cackled Bea. "I wouldn't trust him with my worst enemy."

"To tell you the truth, I don't think I trust him, either," ventured Angela. "I found out something about him that makes me nervous. He's carrying a gun."

"Some of the best people do, Angie," said Bea. She was thinking of Perry. He'd helped her get a gun for herself weeks before, when that pathetic wannabe-thief Cash tried to turn her into his personal meal ticket. At the time, that gun had made Bea feel safe—and helped her get Cash arrested.

"Of course, the gun might mean something more when combined with some of his behavior—like his mysterious ability to snake-charm cops. And his notable nosiness."

"Bea, I'm not joining your cynical party," Angela said. "But you might be right about Foxy. I'm going to check on Connie. I've still got some details to handle for our last event tonight, too."

"We're in the homestretch," said Bea.

"I'll be relieved when it's over. I'm done trying to impress Lee Glastonbury."

"Glad you're coming to your senses, girlie."

"You coming with me?" said Angela, as she turned to head back to the inn.

"I'll be back in a minute. If Pat's game, I thought I'd show her a little more of our grounds."

"Sounds good to me," said Pat.

CHAPTER 18

As soon as Angela was out of earshot, Bea told Pat about her big find in the barn. She dug into her bra to retrieve it, then swiped the padlock symbol—revealing the last photo taken, still showing on the home screen. It was the same one she and Pat had already seen on the latest entry of the troll's blog.

"So here's what I think happened: our troll was hiding out up in the loft, taking pictures with this phone. That would explain how the troll got the pix—by shooting down through the transom windows, from up high in the loft."

Pat's eyes opened wide as she took in a snapshot the phone had captured of the tournament.

"Mind if I take a closer look?"

"Not all. Just show me what you're looking for. Don't forget it should be part of my detective training."

"Well, first of all, we're lucky there's no password on this phone. Check it out, we can get at all the pictures," Pat tilted the phone horizontally and showed Bea several recent pictures they both recognized from the review bomber's blog.

"Check these out. We haven't seen them before." Pat scrolled back through two days' photos and found images of the players arriving—including several showing Frank and James together and Walter and Harry together.

"Is it just me, or does it seem like the players who've been part of this a while—Frank and James, Walter and Harry—don't seem to mix with the more recent crew?"

"I noticed that at breakfast," said Pat. "Could be the ones who've been playing longer have gotten to be more comfortable with each other. Of course, could also mean they're up to something."

"It's poker. Nobody has to be friends. But these people make a point of playing together for three straight days, every year. Odd they've formed little cliques in their small group."

Pat flipped through more photos on the phone. "Well looky here." One of the photos appeared to show two players arguing. They'd stepped away from the nearest light, making it hard to be sure who they were.

"Stupid LED sconces," said Bea. "I knew we should have gone for the old-fashioned energy-hog lights. What do you think? Looks like Walter and James to me."

"They seem mad at each other, whoever they are." One of the men was poking his finger in the face of the other, who had one clenched fist above his head.

"And wait—is that something, or someone, in the bush near them?" The two women tried enlarging the screen, squinting, holding the phone at arm's length—nothing got them any closer to identifying the men in the mystery photo.

"It's no use fighting with this little screen. We need a computer monitor so we can get a closer look," Pat said. "I bet we'll be able to tell who's who once we enlarge the pictures."

"Can you forward that picture to your computer?"

"That's a good idea," Pat said, tapping a few times on the screen to text the photo to her own phone. "Maybe I can download them all onto my computer, though. I've got a cable we can use to attach the phone to my laptop back in my room.

But before we head back to try, mind if I explore where our sneaky shutterbug parked himself?"

Pat hoisted the ladder back up against the barn. Bea held the bottom of the ladder steady as Pat made her way slowly up into the loft. Then Bea used her cane to yank the barn door open and went inside to see what Pat found.

"Seems like he was here a while," Pat said, holding up a few fast-food bags and several bottles filled with brownish-yellow liquid.

"Looks like our stalker was dehydrated," cackled Bea. "I suppose we should thank him for not peeing on the ground in here."

"I'm glad I can call him a guy now without you calling me a sexist. Not a lot of ladies pee into iced tea bottles. It's an endless challenge for us lady PIs when we're on stakeouts."

"You're right. And I believe that means I've helped provide an important clue," said Bea with pride.

"I guess he shot the pictures using his phone through the opening at this end. He could lie down here and aim down at the lobby doors and the ballroom windows." Pat found the hand-fashioned rope near the edge of the loft. "I guess he needed another way out when Billy Ray took the ladder down with him?"

"Yeah, here's what I think happened," said Bea. "I think Billy Ray stumbled onto our junior paparazzo. He'd been getting madder and madder about those pictures. He might have wanted to confront the guy, but we know he was way too drunk for climbing ladders. When Billy Ray fell, our troll must have panicked. He couldn't call the cops without calling attention to himself, trespassing and all. So he figured out how to braid a rope and used it to climb down. Then he rushes out, not realizing he dropped his phone."

"Couldn't this be a crime scene? What if Billy Ray was pushed? Shouldn't Officer McGregor have at least taken a look? Am I right that McGregor didn't even look inside the barn?"

"I think it's possible Officer McGregor is not that great at his job," cackled Bea. "On the other hand, he and the coroner seemed convinced it was an accident. They took a lot of photos and measurements. Didn't seem interested in other evidence."

"They didn't go in the barn at all?"

"That's right. Foxy's supernatural powers of persuasion seemed to take over. McGregor didn't even take fingerprints."

"Maybe not so supernatural. What if the two of

them—Foxy and McGregor—are on the same side?"

"Oooh, conspiracy? I like the way you think, woman. Our case keeps getting juicier!"

"I've been wondering if we should hand over the phone. It could be evidence."

"Here's my thought," said Bea. "Since McGregor didn't even look in the barn, we can always put the phone back where I found it if the coroner decides there might have been foul play. We all saw how hammered Billy Ray was. McGregor seems to have concluded it was an accident. But even if it turns out it wasn't, why shouldn't we keep the phone to work on Betty's review troll mystery—and my detective training? Right? They didn't even look in the place we found it."

"My conscience is clean if yours is. I'll use the ladder to come down, so I don't touch that rope, in the off chance it'll turn out to be evidence, too. Spot me again?"

Bea went back out to hold the ladder while Pat climbed down. Then the two of them heaved the barn door shut, taking care not to touch the handle. As they started to walk away, Pat suggested they take a few minutes to examine for themselves the area where Billy Ray fell. She lifted the ladder off the side of the barn, projecting where it would fall if Billy Ray had leaned back and lost his balance.

"It would depend how high up he'd gotten. But it looks like if he climbed a few rungs, the ladder would have landed right about here when he fell back—more or less where it was found, right?" Pat said, leaning back and letting the ladder fall. "Then he would have fallen right down on the boulder."

"Yep," agreed Bea. "And the way he fell with his head and shoulders resting on the rock doesn't suggest he was pushed, either. Looks too passive."

"No signs of struggle when McGregor flipped him over, right?"

"Correct. And that reminds me—when they rolled Billy Ray over, I noticed something: that classy mistletoe belt buckle of his was gone!"

"Now that's weird. Can't be evidence of a crime, though."

"My thoughts exactly," snorted Bea. "Who would want it?"

CHAPTER 19

That was so close, thought Cash. *Too close!* He was lying on top of the covers of his grubby twin bed after a fitful few hours of sleep, still fully clothed in what he'd worn the night before. He'd even left his dirty sneakers on.

Absently, he ran his fingers around the rim of his unexpected bonus prize: his bodacious mistletoe belt buckle, which he'd jury-rigged onto the waistband of his jeans. He didn't feel bad about stealing it. It was obvious the guy wasn't gonna need it anymore.

Someday, he thought, he'd upgrade his pathetic scooter to a righteous hog. It's damn hard to make a hasty getaway when your ride barely breaks forty miles an hour. One day he'd have a real paint-shaker, with big chrome pipes and ape-hangers. When that day came, the belt buckle would be the first piece of a boss holiday look! He'd get himself an awesome pair of chaps, too.

Picturing himself tearing up the pavement on that hulking bike he coveted—instead of putt-putting around on that weak-ass scooter—was one of his favorite fantasies. But lately, it always ended the same way, with a storm cloud invading his reverie.

Of course, it was all *her* fault. If Betty Snicker-doodle hadn't turned out to be such a crafty old witch, he'd have that sweet ride he deserved already. Instead, he was looking at prison. And he still had no clue how he would pay back that money he borrowed for his bail bond and his lawyer, either.

That's why he had to make Betty pay. He'd put that hag in her place. *She's so full of herself, with her fans and her millions and that loyal babe Angela by her side all the time. Now she's even got that stupid hotel! Stupid fans. Time for them to see the truth.* He laughed, thinking about how he'd turn them all against Betty. *Who's smarter than I am? Nobody! Certainly not that old bag of bones.*

He stared at the peeling ceiling, replaying in his mind the excitement of the night before. *Lucky for me I'm a quick thinker,* he thought, his normal state of grandiose self-love returning. *And lucky for me hay bales have sturdy twine. That rope sure was a brilliant idea. Got a few blisters on my hands, but they'll heal. If I'd called for help getting out of that loft, I'd be back in jail with another trespassing charge on my rap sheet. Hell, they might even call it breaking and entering. Another of those on my record would definitely not be a plus for my trial.*

He rolled off the bed with a groan. Those few hours of sleep weren't enough. Revenge was frickin' exhausting.

Stretching and yawning, he walked the few steps to the sole window of his grim studio. He drew up the narrow, tea-stained shade. A sliver of light streamed in from the alley. *I guess it's still morning,* he thought. Sunshine was piercing the light winter fog, and the trash haulers were doing their noisy thing a few floors below.

He splashed a little water on his face and examined his stubble and dark circles in the grimy mirror. *Man, I need coffee. Now.*

At least I made a good haul before my night's work was short-circuited. But it's not gonna take much longer now, anyway. The plan's gonna start working soon, and Betty will feel the pain. Last night was the best bunch of pictures yet—bet I won't even need any more. Maybe I'll copy them onto my laptop now, before I go grab a cup. It'll be a lot easier to pick and choose the pix on a larger screen.

He set his laptop on the kitchen table and attached a cable to the side, then hit the power button. The hoodie he'd worn the night before was draped over the back of a beat-up old kitchen chair. He grabbed it. Odd. It felt too light. He stuck his hand into the large pocket to retrieve his phone… nothing. He frantically patted his jeans pockets and his shirt.

Nooooooo!

His phone was gone. Did it fall out of his pocket as he slid down that rope? Or while he bent down to pick up the belt buckle? He looked at his trophy again. What was he thinking? It was just a stupid piece of metal.

Now what? He paced the floor and tried to think. *Think!*

Then he remembered something—something useful. Wasn't there software on the phone—an app to let him find it if he lost it?

He sat down in front of his open laptop and looked. Yes, he'd registered the phone. Of course he did, because he was so smart! What a relief. Now he could find the phone—he just had to click open the map….

There it was. The pin on the map showed its location, right smack in the middle of Betty Snickerdoodle's Christmas Inn & Ranch. *Just need to go back to wine country and get it.*

But how could he do that now? In broad daylight? If Betty or anyone in her entourage of losers saw him, they'd call the cops, and he'd be back in jail. He'd have to wait until it was dark again. He'd have to wait until the middle of the night, when no one would notice him, like they hadn't noticed him for two nights in a row.

That might be too late. What if somebody found it in the meantime?

A pop-up window opened. "Is your phone missing?" it asked. "Would you like to lock it?"

Oh, yes, he thought. *Yes, yes I would love to lock it! It was like this website was reading my mind. I'll just lock the phone. Now if one of Betty's eager-beaver minions finds it, they'll get a whole lotta nothing off of it.*

"Enter a message so that someone who finds your phone knows what to do."

Hehehe. Time for a little fun.

He thought a minute, then began to type.

CHAPTER 20

Angela followed unnoticed behind Connie and Foxy as they walked back to the lobby doors. She was deliberately hanging back. Foxy was acting like the perfect gentleman—like a different, reserved, mannerly Foxy. *Huh. Maybe Bea's right,* Angela thought. *The guy's a puzzle.*

As Connie and Foxy made their way in through the lobby, Angela watched them part ways. Connie headed down the hall toward the guest rooms; to Angela's surprise, Foxy didn't escort her. He offered a friendly wave, then headed in the opposite direction—toward the kitchen. What was he up to?

As Foxy rounded the bend and moved out of sight, Angela skipped across the driveway to catch up a bit. She caught a glimpse of his sleek purple shirt as he slipped into the kitchen. She hustled up behind him and peered through the small window of one of the swinging doors. Silently, she watched Foxy open the door of the walk-in cooler, then look back, scanning to make sure no one had spotted him. Angela ducked, hoping he hadn't noticed her. She rose back up slowly and peeped through the window again.

Foxy had pulled the big box with Lee's provisions out of the cooler and set them on the prep table. He was rifling through them, scanning labels and examining the prepped ingredients Chef Ming had left behind.

"Ahem," Angela said, clearing her throat as she entered the kitchen. "Hi, Foxy."

"Angela! I… I didn't see you. What are you doing here?" Foxy was uncharacteristically flustered. "I was just… I guess I just wanted a snack. Thought maybe I'd whip something up."

Angela stared him down, trying to figure him out. Did he expect her to believe this story? The sad part was, she wanted to.

A little monologue played in her head. *Angela Maria Elena!* she hounded herself, channeling her mother's voice. *It's time to act like a manager. It's time to deal with things as they are—not as you wish them to be.*

She took a breath. "Foxy, I'm sure it's obvious guests shouldn't be in a commercial kitchen. Especially when someone recently died after eating food prepared here."

Foxy took a step back. "I suppose you're right. Of course, I didn't mean any harm—"

"It's completely inappropriate. You can't cook in here, anyway. Our insurance policy would never permit that," Angela continued. "I must ask you to leave. And I intend to report this incident to the police—and to Mrs. Glastonbury."

"That's not necessary, is it?" Foxy said. "She'll just get upset over nothing." He was maneuvering toward Angela, attempting to ply her with the charms that had worked so flawlessly over the past few days.

"I'll think about it," said Angela firmly. This time, she wasn't taking the bait. She walked toward the door and reached into the box of leftover breakfast pastries on the shelf next to it.

"Here's a snack," she said, reaching into the box for a muffin. "Please take it and go." She backed up against the door to hold it open for him.

"I'm really sorry, Angela. You know I meant no harm, right?" Foxy smiled weakly, his bravado evaporating. "There's no need to tell Lee I was here, just like I don't need to tell her about the liquor license thing with McGregor, right?"

Was that a threat? thought Angela. *Sounded like a threat.* She looked at him coolly. How could she have been sucked in by his ridiculous charm? Even his designer duds looked smarmy to her now.

"Just *go*, Foxy."

Foxy pressed on. "Speaking of Officer McGregor, I don't suppose he'd be interested in knowing you're hosting an illegal poker tournament here now, would he?"

"Illegal?" croaked Angela.

"Surely you… surely you knew that?"

"Why would I want to host an illegal tournament? And why would you want to be part of one?"

"Law-breaking can be a bit of a thrill, I suppose—right?" said Foxy.

Angela's face froze as she tried to conceal her astonishment. She was most definitely not the kind of person who finds thrills in breaking the law.

"Just. Get. Out. Foxy."

He complied, and she watched him leave,

wishing the door weren't a swinging one so she could give it a good slam.

She wondered what to make of his (empty?) threats, and of the fact that she had just caught him fiddling with the dinner ingredients. Angela stared at the box on the prep table.

Was he looking for something? Or hiding something? He might have been tampering with the ingredients, she thought—despite his protestations. *But how would one tell?* Nervous about the possibilities, she pulled out her cell phone and called her mother.

"Angela? Everything set for tonight? I was about to hit the road. It will take me at least an hour to drive to the inn, and I'd like some extra time to get comfortable in your kitchen."

"I've got another big favor to ask," Angela began. "Is there any way you could bring your own ingredients for tonight?" Then she explained some critical bits she'd left out before—like how a man had died as a result of an allergic reaction.

"So here's the thing. I just found one of the guests in the kitchen, fiddling with the ingredients. Maybe I'm just overly cautious, but what if he put something in the ingredients that caused the other guest's death? And what if he was messing with the ingredients for tonight for similar mischief?"

"Mija… you're making me nervous. Is it safe to even be there?"

"I'm sorry to make you nervous, Mom. I'm sure it's just an abundance of caution on my part. Isn't taking precautions just what a hotel manager is supposed to do?" The fact that the nosy guest also happened to be wearing a gun popped into her head, but Angela knew better than to share that particular detail.

"Don't worry, I'll think of something. Do you mind if I change the menu? I'm thinking prepared salads from a store I love could save time. Can we serve dinner a half hour later?"

"It should be fine. Thank you, Mamá—love you."

"Anything for you, Angelita."

That was the easy part, thought Angela after hanging up. *Now I need to tell Mrs. Glastonbury about the change of dinner plans.* She girded herself —then scolded herself for being so nervous in the first place. She was *managing.* Taking responsibility for her guests' safety. Mrs. Glastonbury should be glad of it, even if things weren't going precisely as she'd expected.

But what to do about Foxy? Could he actually

have meant to harm one of the other players—even deliberately killed him? Her instincts said—shouted—no. She hoped her instincts weren't clouded by Foxy's relentless charm.

Angela decided she knew what to do. She hoped it was the right thing—and for the right reasons. She tapped a number into her cell.

"Mrs. Glastonbury—er, Lee," Angela said. "I've made an adjustment to tonight's dinner. Our new chef is bringing her own ingredients. Yes, I realize it's not what we agreed upon, but I found evidence that the ingredients were tampered with—no, I can't say by whom. But for safety's sake, we're starting fresh. I'm sure you understand."

FOXY SLUMPED against the wall around the corner from the kitchen doors. Good grief. How many more ways could he screw this thing up? At least he felt sure now that Angela had no idea that the poker they were playing could be illegal. That was information he was glad to have.

He walked back out to the lobby and sat in a chair next to the beautifully decorated tree. It reminded him that the second Christmas since he'd concocted his plan was two days away. Two years of painstaking groundwork could be heading down the drain—just when the big prize was in sight. He put his face in his hands and massaged his temples. Get a grip, man.

As he contemplated his next move, Walter walked into the lobby and up to the front desk. Jackson was just hanging up the phone.

"Hi, Jackson."

"Hi—Mr. Wells, isn't it? What can I do for you?"

"Yes, Walter Wells. Can you tell me, is there a business center in the inn? You know, a place with a printer I can use? Hopefully an inkjet? I realize it's a weird request, but I was hoping to print something in color—don't worry, I brought my own ink."

"It's around the far side of the ballroom, near the workout room. If you can wait a few minutes, I'll lead the way. I need to help Ms. Garcia move a heavy box." As he said it, he retrieved a shiny folded dolly from the artfully concealed closet next to the reception desk. The souped-up cart had wheels like small rubber balloons and a handle luxuriously cushioned with suede.

"Posh dolly," said Walter Wells.

"No kidding," laughed Jackson. "The vendor said it's the Rolls Royce of dollies."

"Does it do the heavy lifting, though?" chuckled Foxy, standing up for a closer look.

"Yep, would you believe they say it carries up to 600 pounds?"

Foxy and Walter both nodded, impressed.

Jackson set the dolly on the floor and unfolded the handle. He demonstrated the apparatus by wheeling it about the lobby: "Listen—so quiet, you can't even hear it!"

"Men," said Angela's voice as she rounded the corner. "Are you all fascinated by any sort of mechanical toy?" She was straining to carry a large box. She'd tried to cover it with her sweater, but Foxy noticed it was the box of ingredients Lee Glastonbury had provided—the same box he'd been searching through when Angela caught him in the kitchen.

Jackson rushed to her side. "Let me help you, Ms. Garcia," he said. He took the box from her and put it on the bed of the dolly. "Shall we? Mr. Wells, if you can wait here until I return, I'll show you the way to the business center."

"I'll wait, thank you. I'll grab a cup of coffee from the breakfast room in the meantime."

As Angela and Jackson walked out of sight, Foxy sat back down in his chair. He noticed that instead of getting coffee, Walter took the opportunity for a closer look at the supply closet.

"Nice craftsmanship, huh?"

"It's only a supply closet," Foxy said. "But I guess since you're in real estate, you appreciate these things?"

"Huh? Oh, right, sure," said Walter absently. "It's just interesting that you'd never notice the closet was here. I guess that's why it doesn't have a lock."

"Not too much of value in there. Besides, the front desk is attended most of the time."

"Except overnight."

"I guess you're right," Foxy replied. "Someone could steal a ream of paper or a mop in the middle of the night."

"Just sayin'," said Walter.

"I'm guessing no one in our crowd is a risk for swiping pens and paper clips in the wee hours."

Walter laughed. "I'm sure we've all got bigger fish to fry."

CHAPTER 21

Bea and Pat had a spring in their step as they headed back to their suites to download the rest of the pictures. They were hot on the trail of their troll. Bea was exhilarated.

"Oh no!" she said suddenly, stopping right in her tracks, looking down at the cane she carried, unused, in her left hand. "I can't be seen marching along like this, Pat. I still want to win tonight's tourney." She hastily set the end of her cane back on the ground and leaned theatrically on the handle. "Do you think anyone saw us?"

"I don't think so. Can't hurt to put on a little show, though. Ham it up, girlfriend."

"Good idea!" said Bea. "Walk ahead of me a bit."

Bea waited a few beats until Pat was several yards away, then staggered. She dropped to the ground and began to wail melodramatically.

"Oh no, Pat, my trick knee again! It must be my rheumatism!" She was yelling loud enough now that most of Napa County could hear her. "Help me, Pat, please! Help me back up!"

"Hold on, Bea!" Pat said. "I'm coming to help!" Then she loped toward her pupil as if moving in slow motion through an invisible ocean. "There we go, my friend. Let's get you upright. Steady now." She was right next to Bea, but yelled as if she were still at least ten yards from her.

"Oh, thank you, dear, dear Pat," Bea shouted. She was on her feet again but not quite vertical, hunching over as she leaned on her cane.

Pat looped Bea's free hand through her arm. "Let me help you along, Bea," she announced loudly. "Now let's make our way *very* carefully back to your suite."

The two limped along at a snail's pace, the remaining few yards to the inn's entrance promising to take an eternity.

"Good grief, this is tedious," hissed Bea under her breath. "I'm dying to get a look at those photos. It's our big detecting breakthrough!"

"Do you want to win that tourney? Because any of your competitors could be watching—"

"I know, I know."

The two arrived at their adjoining suites. "I need to use the loo, then I'll be right in to check out the pictures with you."

"Sounds like a plan. I need to hit the head, too," said Pat. "Then I'll get started on the download."

Inside her suite, Bea was overjoyed to see a housekeeper had already tidied everything up. Her "FUDGING LOVE CHRISTMAS" sweater was placed with care on the bed, as if it were made of the finest cashmere. She turned on the bathroom light and noticed it, too, had been immaculately cleaned. A delicate lemon scent hung in the air, and the fixtures sparkled.

Bea was still using the bathroom when she heard a shout from Pat's suite.

"Oh no!"

"What?"

"It looks like we're out of luck," Pat yelled back. "The troll has locked down his phone."

"How'd he do that if we've got the phone?"

"Must be an app on the phone. There are apps that let you log in from any computer and turn your phone into a useless toy."

Bea washed her hands and walked through the adjoining door to join Pat. "Any idea who owns it?"

"That's the worst part. There's a message on the screen. Take a look—it seems it's a pre-paid cell. That would make it untraceable."

Bea walked up behind Pat, who was seated at her desk fiddling with the phone. As she peered over Pat's shoulder, she suddenly let out a shriek of laughter.

"Because 'Cash only?' Bwahahaha!" Bea her shoulders were shaking, like they always did when she was enjoying a hysterical laugh.

"Pardon me, lady, but what's so funny?"

"Do you think the cell provider would put four exclamation points after 'cash only'?" asked Bea. The message on the phone read:

IF YOU FIND THIS PHONE LEAVE IT WHERE YOU FOUND IT

CASH ONELY!!!!

DON'T STEAL IT OR YOUR IN TROUBLE

Pat spun in her chair and looked at her gleeful elder apprentice. "Come to think of it, I'd have also thought they'd know how to spell 'only.' But I still don't get why you're laughing so hard."

Bea roared even louder with laughter.

Pat sighed and waited.

"OK, OK, I'll tell you. I know who our troll is! But first, join me in a happy dance!" She coaxed Pat out of her chair, and the two spun around in a circle, Pat wearing an indulgent, confused expression on her face.

Winded, Bea plopped down on the bed and explained to Pat how the phone had to belong to Cash—the dimwitted thief who'd tried to get rich by stealing a Betty manuscript a few months before. As she concluded her story, her tone grew sober.

"Sometimes, life seems truly unfair," said Bea, making an effort to sound solemn.

"You mean because he's after you again? I was wondering why you didn't sound more scared. It's no joke, Bea. This guy attacked you and broke into your house."

"Yeah," Bea replied, holding her head down, looking serious. "It's truly unfair because I had so much fun crushing him the first time, I can't believe I get to do it again!" She was cackling with abandon now, slapping her knee as she always did at her own jokes. "Can you believe how dumb that guy is—trying to scare us with that message?" She was getting winded from laughing so hard.

"You had me going there, Bea."

"Sorry. I love pulling off a good bluff."

"How is it he's back on your trail? Out on bail?"

"Yep. But here's the best part. He's not allowed to go anywhere near me. Just turning up here is enough to put him back in the can. Probably with new charges, too. He is such a birdbrain! No wait —that's an insult to birds!

"I've got a way to stop him—and get all of his photos, too. We'll need Aseem's help," Bea said. She called Aseem on the internet tube and asked him to join them.

"While we wait for him, we've still got that photo I texted to myself," said Pat. "Let's try to figure out who those two dudes are." She picked up her own phone to send the image to her computer.

"Three dudes, don't forget," said Bea. "There's that shadow in the bush. Someone is spying on them. Maybe they're a trio of cheaters worried about who's double-crossing who. I've encountered some poker cheats in my time. Nobody is more paranoid about being cheated than a cheater."

"Let's take a closer look."

CHAPTER 22

"You all set, Ms. Garcia?" Jackson had wheeled the dolly into Angela's suite and was placing the heavy box on her desk.

"I am, thank you, Jackson—and please don't forget, you can call me Angela, at least when no guests are around, for sure."

"Will do, Ms. Gar—er, Angela," Jackson said with a smile as he folded up the dolly and carried it away.

Angela pulled her sweater off the top of the box. Where to start? She wasn't even sure she knew the difference between cilantro and cinnamon.

Angela hadn't inherited her mother's culinary flair, nor had she embraced Maria's many attempts to teach her. She was always too busy building her marketing business—and now she was even busier, working on becoming a full-fledged media mogul. Plus, one of her mother's fantastic home-cooked meals could be had for the price of a drive to Sacramento almost any time she wanted. She suspected that was why her mother stopped pushing the issue. Mouthwatering home-cooked dinners were a reliable way to make sure she got to see her only daughter now and then.

Let's see, does any of this stuff look like it's been tampered with? Angela thought. Flummoxed about where to start, she decided she'd roughly sort dessert ingredients from dinner ones. She could do that even with her complete lack of cooking knowledge. Like, say, this bag of chopped onions —easily classified as a dinner ingredient.

She held the gallon bag up to the light. *Yep, looks like onions to me,* she shrugged. *But how can I tell if it's been doctored?* Angela noticed a milky liquid in the bottom. Could be onion juice. Could be lethal poison. She had to laugh—she was the last person who'd know the difference.

When she turned the bag around, she saw that the chef had labeled it with a marker: "diced onions, dinner, night two –Ming." That confirmed what it was for. And Angela had to assume it had started out as just an innocent bag of onions. But had Foxy—or anyone else—done anything to it? *It looks fine to me,* she shrugged. *But who knows?*

Angela was discouraged, but too curious to give up. She pulled more ingredients from the box and noticed that some were separated into a tray within the box.

As she lifted the tray out of the box and onto the desk, she spotted a sticky note on the side. In handwriting different from the chef's, the note on the tray said "Important: dessert ingredients for night one." Huh. Presumably, Lee's writing.

She picked the biggest item out of the tray—the gluten-free flour canister Chef Ming had shown her in the kitchen. It was large but light; although its lid said ten pounds, it was more than half-empty. The antique-style decoration on the outside of the container proclaimed it "Napa Mills Old-Fashioned Pastry Flour, Now 100% Gluten-Free."

Under that headline was another sticky note in Lee's hand: a large one, reminding the chef that "this flour must be used for night one dessert." Angela noticed that Lee had taken the extra step of taping down the unglued side of the sticky note. Curious, she picked at the edge of the tape with her fingernail and peeled it back. The note concealed information on the canister that might have been important:

"Attention: Not an Allergen-Free Food. Please see bottom label for allergy information."

Angela held the canister overhead to read the allergy information. Small traces of adhesive still clung to the metal, but the label was gone. The company's website address was stamped on the container, though. Angela switched on her laptop and entered the company's URL, then clicked on the page for gluten-free pastry flour.

"Napa Mills' Gluten-Free Pastry Flour is our proprietary formulation. It contains no grains nor any other sources containing gluten. We've put our expert bakers to the test and they've come up with a baking flour so good, you'll never believe it's gluten-free! And it's simple to use, too: just measure and use it like any cake flour."

The enticing description sat above a gallery of images of delicious-looking baked goods—all supposedly made with Napa Mills' gluten-free flour. But underneath the pretty pictures, in fine print, was another message:

"Important note for consumers allergic to nuts and legumes, and the chefs who serve them: this flour is guaranteed free of gluten, but contains almond, lupine, and soy flours, all of which may cause life-threatening reactions in people allergic to tree nuts, peanuts, and other legumes."

Perhaps this was the sort of information that was on the canister's missing label, Angela thought. *But who removed it?* The most obvious candidate was Mrs. Glastonbury. Foxy had the opportunity, too, though. Maybe he had been covering her—or their—tracks.

There was that ever-present friction between them, though. Then again, if you wanted to hide the fact you were allies, acting like you didn't get along would be a logical tactic.

~

I MIGHT BE GETTING TOO old for this poker thing, Walter thought as he walked silently with Jackson to the business center. *I'll tell Lee this will be my last one. Or maybe I'll stick with it for Gstaad in January—and then maybe the Caymans in February. Oh, and Monaco will be lovely in May. She may be annoying sometimes—ok, all the time—but she sure picks pretty hives to attract rich bees. With all those fabulous tax havens to choose from, why'd she have to pick this horrible little place? I knew it would be a problem somehow.*

Almost on cue, the phone in his pocket buzzed with a familiar tone. *Lee.* Walter hung back a bit, letting Jackson walk ahead as he answered it with a blunt "yes."

"I know I overreacted before. Now you're doing the same. We shouldn't make the same mistake twice. Yes, I recognize that what I did can't be taken back! Acting in haste now won't change that, and could be just as bad. Nothing can tie us to—er, you-know-what." He had lowered his voice to an urgent hiss.

"Why aren't you relieved? If anything, that call you got seems to suggest suspicion in another direction. No, I have no idea who was seen in the kitchen. But I'll make sure it wasn't one of us."

As he approached a corner, Jackson politely slowed down to let Walter catch up. Walter stopped to finish his call, lowering his voice, worried that Jackson might overhear.

"Listen, I have to go," he said, at a normal volume. "One of the staff is kindly showing me to the business center, and I'm being terribly rude. I'll talk to you later."

"I hope you didn't hang up on my account," Jackson said.

"Don't worry, it was no one I can't call back."

"Well, we're here—our little business center. You can see it's not large, but we put a lot of effort into outfitting it. You use your card key to enter, like this."

Jackson opened the door and revealed a compact office with a computer, printer, scanner/fax, speakerphone, and a tidy cabinet packed with various office supplies.

"Since most people have laptops these days, we assumed what guests want from a place like this is printing, faxing, and add-ons you can't easily bring with you—so that's what you see here. You can also hook up to super-fast wired internet if you need to work with large files."

"I guess I'm like everyone else, then," said Walter. "I really just need to print my boarding pass." But as he said it, he was checking on the scanner in detail.

"Great, well I'll leave you then to check out what we have here. Feel free to call me at the front desk or drop by if you need help."

Jackson shut the door behind him as he left.

Walter took his cell out of his pocket and hit redial.

"Listen, I still think it would be wrong to overreact. We could blow up everything over nothing! But if we have to activate the nuclear option, we've got everything we need." Walter had his phone tucked under his cheek and was inspecting the workings of the printer while he talked.

"Mr. Wells?" said Jackson, popping his head back in through the door. "Sorry to interrupt your call. I remembered you said that you brought your own color ink. The printer's loaded up with it already, so no need to supply any." It occurred to Jackson that printing a boarding pass seemed a little weird. But what business was it of his?

Walter tapped the mute button on the phone a little harder than necessary. "Yes, I can see that. Thanks." He shut the lid of the printer.

"No problem, Mr. Wells," said Jackson amiably, closing the door again behind him.

Walter waited a few seconds until he felt sure Jackson was gone, then unmuted the phone. "I'm back. No, there's nothing to worry about. If it becomes necessary, we can do everything we need to do right here."

CHAPTER 23

"Boop-boop-boop. Angela calling," said the internet tube in Bea's suite.

"What's up, Angie?"

"Lots," said Angela. Then she told Bea how she'd run into Foxy nosing around in the kitchen. "You were right, Bea. He's not trustworthy. I think I might have been blinded by his charm, at least a little."

"You know I'd never say 'I told you so,' girlie," Bea replied. That was, of course, a blatant lie, even if Bea actually believed it when she said it.

"My mom's brought her own ingredients. She's getting started in the kitchen."

"Your mother's a woman of many talents. And she sure loves you!"

"Believe me, I know how lucky I am right about now."

"Have you told Bossybritches yet?"

"Yep. She didn't like it. But it's not her decision. It's up to the inn to protect its guests."

"Now that sounds like the strong Angie I know and love."

"Would you believe the earth did not stop rotating on its axis because Lee Glastonbury was disappointed?"

"She'd be even more disappointed to know you're onto her. She's one of those people who uses being permanently annoyed as a way to get what she wants."

"I'm glad we have a contract," Angela laughed. "And I'm even gladder she prepaid 50% of it. And —above all—I'm glad tonight is our last tournament."

"Amen to that, sister. I'm glad I've still got one more chance to win one of these suckers. By the way, Perry and I figure some players are cheating."

"Are you sure?"

"We saw it happen. And Perry was planning to confirm with video—I think he might even have done that already," Bea fibbed.

Bea decided it was best not to tell Angela about Aseem's video recording failing two nights in a row. Perry told her that Aseem was really embarrassed about the whole thing. Bea thought if Angela knew, it might crush the poor guy's confidence. Besides, it was entirely possible—even probable—that the videos weren't failing, but were sabotaged.

"We've got a plan to throw a monkey wrench into their little scam tonight. It'll be fun, girlie!" Bea said. "Somebody's going to be taught a nice lesson."

Angela instinctively opened her mouth to protest that it might disrupt the evening, then realized she was falling right back into her people-pleasing habits. "I'll look forward to seeing that play out," she said instead. "Please be careful. There's something else we need to talk about—something I found in the kitchen."

She then gave Bea the highlights of how she became suspicious about the flour, and how she came to suspect Lee, or Foxy—or both—might have been behind a deliberate poisoning of Eddie.

"I called Officer McGregor," Angela said. "He didn't take the possibility of Foxy being involved too seriously. But he said he'd come by in the morning to pick up the flour and other ingredients as possible evidence. He also said he could send over the detail cop that Perry knows to provide a little extra security tonight if we want." She decided not to mention what Foxy had said about the tournament being illegal—not to McGregor, naturally, nor to Bea. At the moment, she preferred not to acknowledge the possibility the inn was hosting a felony.

"Oh good," said Bea. "Aseem is helping me and Pat tonight with a side project. We think we figured out who has been posting those pictures and reviews. We want to catch him in the act. Aseem's on the case. The cop could stand in Aseem's place by the control room while the door's open for the games."

"It won't be dangerous, will it, Bea? I mean, whoever it is seems to just sneak around taking pictures, but they are doing it in the middle of the night."

"Don't you worry about your boyfriend, girlie."

"He's not my boyfriend."

"I still think you have a shot—even though you haven't been treating him so great since Mr. Fancypants got here. Everyone's noticed how googoo-eyed you've been around Foxy, especially Aseem."

"You're imagining Aseem cares about that," Angela said. She managed a neutral tone of voice, even though she was mortified by fresh memories of her silly behavior with Foxy.

"I think Aseem wants a chance to impress you, Angie—and I think you're gonna be impressed."

"He's a grown man. He can do what he wants. Just promise me… promise you… oh, never mind!"

"You're right. He's a grown man. Besides, Perry is lending him his gun."

"What?!"

"Don't worry so much, girlie! Perry had time to give him a lesson on using it this afternoon."

This only made Angela worry more, but there was no time to discuss it.

"There's more I want to talk to you about, Bea. Based on my research, it looks like Eddie was poisoned on purpose. And I'm still looking into a few other clues. But we've got to get ready for tonight, and I've still got to make sure my mom has everything she needs in the kitchen."

"Pat, Perry, Aseem, and I are planning to meet after the tournament to compare notes. We're meeting at Aseem's casita, to stay out of range of prying eyes and ears. Join us?"

"Sounds like a plan."

The tube disconnected the call and Angela ran through what she had to do next: shower, hair, makeup, dress, check in with Maria about dinner, get the detail cop into position. A long list, and she wasn't long on time.

She pulled the third of Bea's gift dresses out of her closet: the black sequined sheath with the low-cut back. She hadn't planned it, but it turned out she'd worn the dresses in perfect order. Unlike the other two, this one hadn't a whiff of cuteness or girliness or flirtiness. It was unmistakably an adult woman's dress.

After a quick shower, Angela did her makeup and blew out and pinned her hair into a voluminous half-up, half-down style. She put on her dress and the stilettos and added sparkling chandelier earrings.

Standing in front of the mirror, she appraised her appearance:

Fancy? Check.

Grown up? Check.

Ready? Check.

She grabbed the tiny black satin clutch in which she stowed her room key and her lipstick, then headed out the door to see how Maria was doing with dinner.

~

"LISTEN UP, EVERYONE," pronounced Bea from on high.

Just as the final night's tournament was about to start, Perry and Pat had helped her climb to a precarious perch on one of the chairs. Now Bea was resting one hand on Perry's shoulder to steady herself. Pat was tapping on a water glass to get everyone's attention.

"Before we get started, I'd like to announce a few changes to our rules for tonight," Bea began.

Across the room, Lee's head whipped around to see how on earth such an announcement could be happening. Having just finished more or less reiterating the rules she'd established for the prior two nights' events, she was visibly offended. Of course, for Bea, displeasing Lee was part of the fun. Bea grinned as she glimpsed Angela's beautiful face and saw she was enjoying the moment as well.

"It has come to my attention that some players have had concerns about conduct—dare I say, even possible collusion or even *cheating* in the tournament."

Now it was Foxy's turn to react, his jaw dropping open at Bea's brazen insinuation. He looked at her and waited for the other shoe to drop.

"I'm not accusing anyone of anything. And I

won't put anyone in an awkward position by revealing who among us thought something unsavory might be going on. We all already know, though, that some qualms were expressed by poor, departed Billy Ray.

"As your host and the owner of this fine establishment, I feel obligated to make sure everyone's comfortable with the game. We're playing for a whole lotta cabbage here! I know, I know—we can all afford it. But since the competition's the thing, everybody still wants to be sure they have a chance to win fair and square, right?

"I do hope you're not getting upset, Lee," Bea said, her tone turning unnaturally sweet. "I hope it's unlikely that any cheating has occurred. A few safeguards will simply reassure all of us. And rest assured, the measures we'll follow are consistent with the rules of the World Series of Poker and the tournament directors' association."

Mrs. Glastonbury wasn't taking Bea's patronizing well. Her face had gone almost scarlet and her lips were tightly pursed. But she could hardly object to what Bea was announcing.

"Here's what we're going to do," Bea said. She explained that seat assignments would be drawn using Perry's tournament seat cards—not the assignments predetermined by Lee. Perry placed the seat cards upside down on the felt and scrambled them for a minute to be sure they were randomized. Each player grabbed a card. Several exchanged looks when they learned where they'd be sitting. Perry flipped over the last card which would be Bea's: seat #1, right next to the dealer. Foxy would sit to her left in seat #2.

Bea explained that chip counts would be confirmed by Perry and the dealer before and after each break, "to ensure stack integrity." She suspected she was on the right track when she noticed a couple of the players she suspected of cheating looking down as she spoke.

"Lastly, we'll be using these brand-new, custom-made Christmas-themed cards and chips for our play tonight. Aren't they pretty?" A dealer wheeled in a small cart containing all the chips, divided into individual stacks that were still shrink-wrapped, just as the cards were.

"As you can see," Bea continued, "It will be clear to all of us exactly how many of each denomination will be in play. No one but Perry has had access to these decks." The dealer distributed chip stacks to all eight players and shuffled one of the fresh decks.

"With that, Perry, shall we shuffle up and deal?"

"Sure, but we've got to get you into your seat first." He stood in front of her chair so she could place both hands on his shoulders, then he surprised her by reaching under her arms and picking her up, then gently placing her on her feet.

"Watch your hands, sir!" said Bea.

"Oh no, I'm sorry!"

"Just kidding," said Bea with a devious laugh. "My boobs left that neighborhood years ago."

Remembering her persona for the table, he passed her cane to her, and she resumed her fragile posture. He leaned over and whispered in her ear, "Remember, you're frail. And now I really like your chances. Sure you don't want to sell me a stake?"

When everyone was seated, Perry announced the starting blinds and instructed the dealer to "put the cards in the air." The dealer started the game. After a few hands, everyone settled into a quiet, comfortable rhythm.

"Got a rush coming on, Betty?" said Foxy. After an hour of play, Bea and Foxy were in a hand together, and Bea had just called his huge raise. The pot was by far the biggest of the night.

"How did you know?" said Bea, flipping over two aces. "Two aces plus the one on the board makes three!" she said gaily. "Oh, and I guess with that pair on the board, I've got a full house. What you got, Foxy Fox?"

Foxy didn't answer, just threw his hand into the pile of discarded cards.

"One of those poker books I've been reading said that if I call you, I get to see your hand. Isn't that right, dealer?"

"Strictly speaking, that's true," said the dealer. "But once a player's cards are in the muck, there's no way to retrieve them."

"Ooh, you're one trickster fox, Foxy," laughed Bea. "Does that mean you were bluffing?" Foxy shrugged and smirked. It didn't matter to Bea. She'd figured out he was bluffing from the first bet. She'd asked to see his hand just for grins, to see his reaction. Foxy was at best a mediocre poker player—but Bea was positive he didn't know that.

The dealer pushed the huge pile of chips in Bea's direction, and she began organizing and stacking them in the slow, inexpert manner of an amateur. There was little need to persist with the ruse. With the cheating contained, and a sprinkle of luck, she was eliminating her competitors in a systematic fashion.

"Hahaha!" Bea roared with laughter as she

raked another huge pot, slapping the table and disrupting the quiet atmosphere of the room.

"I'm so sorry," she said, catching her breath. "Sometimes I forget how much fun playing cards can be. You'd never know it from all the long faces around here, though."

CHAPTER 24

I guess I shouldn't wear my tux tonight, Aseem thought. *Who knows what kind of mess I could end up getting into?*

He debated whether he should even take a shower, but he decided he'd better in the end. What if he ended up dead, or in the hospital? Like his mum had always said, if the worst happens, you should at least be clean.

Besides, he couldn't get into position until it had been dark a while. He couldn't help being antsy, though. He was on another bad streak, with all those annoying problems with the video. It bugged him that he still couldn't figure out why the recordings were failing. If he succeeded, this little stakeout could make up for a lot of mistakes.

Might take some of Angela's attention away from that annoying Foxworth guy, too.

Let go of that, he reminded himself. He knew he should be happy for her if she finds someone else. That Foxy, though. Ugh. Slippery, to say the least. A rich jerk who acts like everything in the world is his for the taking. How many broken hearts has Foxy left in his wake? He didn't want hers to be next.

Aseem looked down at the revolver in its shoulder holster, laid out flat on his bed. He picked it up gingerly and reviewed all the steps Perry told him about how to use it. He released the cylinder and examined it: six bullets, all still there.

Aseem took the bullets out, then practiced the stance that Perry taught him. Holding a real gun wasn't much like he'd expected. He thought it would be more like a video game. Would he do everything right in the heat of the moment? Hadn't Perry said pulling the gun out would probably do the job on its own? Shooting it would almost certainly be unnecessary. Better to practice again, anyway. Better safe than sorry.

He showered and put on jeans, a clean shirt, and a thick fleece hoodie. It might be a long, cold wait in that barn. Besides being warm, the thick fleece kept the holster—and the extra cell phone he was carrying—hidden from view.

It was well past dark now. He stuck a candy bar in his pocket, grabbed a bottle of water, and headed out the door. As he walked to the barn from the casita, he envisioned confronting Cash. This improved his mood considerably. He savored the scene as it played out in his mind's eye. It was going to be so good!

Whenever he remembered how he'd fallen for Cash's get-rich-quick scheme, he felt like such a dupe. He couldn't have known at the time that Cash's plan involved Bea and Angela—he didn't even realize Bea was Betty Snickerdoodle back then. But now he knew, with hindsight, that he could have unwittingly helped Cash harm his friends—and it made him really angry.

I'm not a vengeful guy, thought Aseem, *but I'm starting to see how people get that way. It would be awesomely satisfying to be the guy that stopped that jerk this time.*

The thrilling upside of the plan filled him with nervous energy. He tried telling himself to calm down. In all likelihood, he'd be waiting for hours for Cash to come back for that phone. If he didn't figure out how to relax, he might have an adrenaline crash just when it was time for action.

Finally, he walked out into the starry night toward the barn. *The tournament must be underway now,* he thought, noticing the crystalline lights through the transom windows of the ballroom. Just as Bea said to, he avoided the handle of the door, instead drawing it back by grasping the side of the wood panel itself.

Inside, it was just as she described. The grassy pile was there, in the darkness at the far end of the barn, with the hand-braided rope dangling down from the loft. He dropped the phone onto the mound of straw. Then he found a spot in the nearest corner, behind a bunch of old equipment, where he would sit and wait. When Cash came to retrieve the phone, he'd come right up behind him with the gun. Perfect set-up.

He moved into the corner and tried to settle in. Should he stand there in the shadows? He tried sitting down on an old pail. Not bad, but would he be able to spring to his feet fast enough? He decided he could. As long as he listened for sounds outside the barn, he'd have time to react.

Well good, glad that's settled, he thought. He sighed. *How much longer,* he wondered? *I'm bored already.* He pulled out his cell phone and looked at the time: 12 minutes had passed since he left the casita. It was shaping up to be a long night.

He supposed he could eat the candy bar now. No, better to save it for later. *So bored,* he thought with a sigh. *So... bored.*

He looked up at the loft. Was that where Cash took pictures for his lousy blog? How would that work? Curiosity crept into his bored brain.

I wonder if I can climb up there, he thought—*just for a minute.* Pat said the pictures were taken much later at night. There had to be plenty of time still. Why not take a look? Surely there'd be time to hustle back down if he heard someone coming. But how to get up there?

Aseem peeked outside the barn door and saw the ladder lying on the ground. *I see,* he thought: *you're supposed to climb that ladder up to those second-story doors.* But if he tried that he might be seen, even from a distance, if Cash were to show up unexpectedly while he climbed. If he moved the ladder inside, Cash might notice it missing and suspect something was up. Bea had told him to leave things as Cash would expect to find them.

Maybe there's another way up. He reached up and confirmed the loft was up too high to touch with his hand. He dragged the pail over from the corner and flipped it upside down. Standing on it, the underside of the loft was still out of reach of his fingers.

The rope Cash had fashioned caught Aseem's eye again. *I wonder if it's thick enough to climb up,* he thought. *If I can shinny up a foot or two, I could pull myself onto the loft.* He decided to give it a try.

He grabbed the rope and began to pull himself up. *Not bad,* he thought. *Maybe climbing that fake rock wall at the gym has value after all. Too bad this rope is so skinny and frayed, though. It's already cutting into my hand.*

After a few repetitions of hoisting his feet up, wrapping the rope in place around them, then pushing further up the rope, he rolled onto the loft. *Yes!*

And then, his reward. He looked out of the loft door and saw what Cash had been after: a clear view of the inn's entrance, the driveway, and the ballroom windows. The drapes were drawn, but useless to prevent Cash's spying. The loft provided an excellent view into the ballroom through the transom windows. He saw the players seated around the main tournament table. Angela and Lee Glastonbury stood off to the side. Lee looked cranky, as usual, but it seemed Angela was once more managing to placate the annoying battle-ax. Her ability to juggle it all amazed him—and her beauty took his breath away. He smiled. She has no idea how incredible she is.

Lost in that thought, Aseem didn't notice the sound of a scooter moving up the road near the inn. He heard the muffled sound of feet on the grass nearby and he realized Cash was coming. Now what? If he climbed down now, he might not get back into his corner in time. Cash might see him and run.

Too late now. A tall figure moved through the door. Aseem scuttled back from the edge of the loft, hoping he was hidden from view, and pulled the gun out of the holster. Lying on his belly, he peered down into the barn. He watched Cash anxiously scan the barn floor, then smile as he spotted the phone and reached down to pick it up.

"Don't move, Cash. I'd like to say it's nice to see you, but... no."

Cash froze for a moment. Still hunched over, phone in hand, he turned his head toward Aseem.

"Oh, it's you, Cash said. "Still looking for your big break, huh? Tech thing still not working out for you?"

Aseem pointed the gun at Cash. "I see the crime thing's still not working out for you. Put your hands against the wall and don't move. Then I'll come down and explain how this is going to go." Aseem was glad for the dim light. Hopefully

Cash couldn't see how much his hand was shaking.

Cash moved toward the wall and did as he was told. But then he changed his mind and reached down instead. "I don't think so, Aseem." He picked up the pail and tossed it at Aseem's face.

"You're an idiot," Aseem said, thinking fast. He ducked the pail and scrambled off the loft, landing on top of Cash and pinning him to the ground on his stomach. The gun landed about a foot away. Cash tried to grab it, but Aseem rewarded him by leaning on his arm with all his weight, jamming his elbow into the barn's hard dirt floor.

"Owww!" wailed Cash.

Aseem stretched his arm out and snagged the gun. He poked the nose of it into Cash's back.

"And here I was planning to offer you a stay-out-of-jail-free card. Maybe you'd like to tell me why I shouldn't change my mind. Because it will only take one quick call to the police and you'll be right back in jail, genius."

CHAPTER 25

Bea was strutting about with even more spirit than usual. It was past midnight, and though she'd complained about various aches and pains all night at the table, she was miraculously doing without her cane as she milled among the players in the ballroom.

"So Lee," she said, grabbing the client's arm with inappropriate familiarity, "I guess we should fill everyone in on the plan for the cash awards tomorrow. Mind if I do the honors?"

"Of course," Lee hissed through gritted teeth. "As you made clear earlier this evening, your house, your rules."

"Why thank you, Lee. Listen up, everyone."

The players gathered round and stood in a semicircle for Bea's announcement.

"It's late, so I'll be brief. As Lee said on the first night, tomorrow morning will be the awards ceremony, where the prizes will be presented to the three winners—James, Walter, and yours truly." Bea dramatically pointed at herself with her thumbs, the fresh irritation on Lee's face only sweetening the moment. Angela and Perry were applauding enthusiastically. Bea thought for a moment she saw Walter and James exchange anxious glances. Everyone else looked ready for bed.

"We'll have breakfast here in the ballroom tomorrow as part of the festivities. Lee asked that we start by 8:30AM, so please don't be late. There's still time for us all to get our beauty sleep. You won't want to miss the special treats we have planned for our last morning together."

Rex and Max and their glamourous, silent girlfriends were the first to say good night, genially promising to "attend the morning fun," despite no claim to any winnings.

Lee followed right behind. She left without saying good night to anyone. "Don't let the door hit your butt on the way out, Lady G!" hollered Bea. Angela shook her head at Bea's rudeness, but kept on smiling.

Walter, Harry, James, and Frank stood together, apart from everyone else and close to the ballroom's French doors—the ones that led out to the patio. The moonlight was still streaming in through the transom windows, although the heavy drapes still blocked the doors entirely.

"I'll see you all in the morning," said James. "Looking forward to collecting my winnings." Bea thought he didn't sound all that excited. Could Foxy have been right that the winnings weren't important to her opponents? *Nah,* she thought. Walter followed James out with a friendly wave to the room.

"Shame we had to leave the drapes shut," said Frank. He was lifting the drapes of one door and quickly scanning beneath them. "We missed a beautiful night sky." Bea noticed—and saw that Pat had, too—that he seemed to be trying a little too hard to look casual.

"Take a walk outside. Still plenty of moonlight to enjoy," Bea said. "Just don't stay up too late. We wouldn't want you to miss our last time together tomorrow morning."

"You can count on it," Frank said. He dropped the drape and left the room with Harry. Foxy followed shortly after, pausing to say goodnight to Angela.

Once the players and Lee had cleared out, Bea reminded Pat, Perry, and Angela to head over to Aseem's casita, where they'd be unlikely to be overheard as they compared notes.

"We'll each head down separately, so no inquiring minds get any ideas. Angie, you head down now. Aseem should be back but, in case he's still working on his little errand, you can use your master key to let yourself in.

"Perry, you follow next. Pat and I have a little dodge planned to make sure our neighbors don't suspect we're up to something."

Bea left the ballroom after Perry and walked the short distance to her suite and Pat's. Their rooms were right near four of the players', plus Mrs. Glastonbury's. Bea wanted to be sure all of them heard her arrive back at her suite.

"Stupid contraption!" Bea complained in a loud voice, pretending the cardkey had failed. She gave the door a few good poundings with her cane, then used the key to open the door. "Finally!" she exclaimed. "I'm in!"

Pat waited a few minutes, as they'd agreed, and locked up the ballroom's hallway doors. Then she arrived at her door and contrived a similar fuss. When she finally opened her door, Bea was standing just inside. Bea slipped out the door, then Pat stuck her head into the suite, yawned as loudly as possible and yelled "can't wait to get to bed," then crept back out before forcefully shutting the door from the outside. The two ladies gave each other a silent thumb's up. Then they took off their shoes and tiptoed down the hall to the side exit.

They snuck through the grounds to Aseem's casita. When they arrived, they were relieved to find Perry and Angela had made it there unnoticed.

"Where's Aseem?" said Angela. "Shouldn't he be back by now?"

"Don't worry, girlie. He's only dealing with Cash. Aseem could outsmart him while in a coma. Cash probably just arrived later than we expected."

"Wait, what? Aseem is dealing with *Cash?* Crazy, criminal Cash? How could you not have mentioned that?!"

Oops, thought Bea. *I suppose all would soon be revealed, anyway.* "I didn't want to worry you prematurely."

"That guy's unhinged on a good day. And now he hates you more than ever! I guess I see now why Aseem needed a gun! Honestly, how could you, Bea?"

"Did you not remind me earlier that Aseem is a grown man? A man who, I might add, has his own reasons for wanting to deal with Cash himself."

"But how? How will he deal with Cash?"

"Aseem will tell you all about it when he comes back. No reason to steal his thunder. In the meantime, why don't you tell us what you've discovered?"

Angela sighed. "OK. Why don't I start with what I learned about the flour that Lee insisted we use for the dessert on night one?"

FACED with the prospect of returning to jail—or worse, getting shot—Cash decided to do the sensible thing for once.

He followed Aseem to the business center, where they would download and remove all the pictures off his phone, erase his snarky reviews, take his spiteful little blog offline (assigning the web address to Aseem), and transfer ownership of his phone to Aseem. Aseem took pictures of everything with his own phone, for extra proof. And he got a few choice shots of Cash for good measure.

"But I'm riding a crap scooter all the way from

wine country to the Tenderloin in the middle of the night," moaned Cash. "You can't leave me without a phone."

"Stop crying, you big baby," Aseem said. "There's no way you're getting this phone back. But you can take this fresh pay-as-you-go phone I've got right here." He reached onto a shelf in the business center and pulled out a new phone, still sealed in its box. "You'll have to alert all your friends that you've got a new number, but I can't imagine that will take very long. It's even got some minutes pre-loaded.

"We're just about done here, finally, so let's recap our deal. You will never, ever post another thing about Betty. And you're never going to come near the inn or anyone associated with it ever again. In return for this—which you were supposed to be doing anyway as part of your bail, idiot—we'll forget about this little incident. Oh, and you can even keep that tacky belt buckle if you want."

"Fine. Can I go now?"

"You're not very grateful. You've just received a gift. A very generous gift. Let's hear a proper thank you."

"Thank you," Cash grunted. "Happy now?"

"Pretty happy. But let's do one more thing."

Aseem called up Betty's book sales page on the computer and told Cash to log in.

"First, click on the five stars. Yes, that's it. Now write something heartfelt about how Betty's books have changed your life."

"Come on!"

"Do it."

Aseem ignored the multiple errors in Cash's two-sentence review of *Treacle Town ♥ Christmas.* He was already tired of the project after listening to Cash whine about it for 15 straight minutes. He instructed Cash to change the email address associated with the account to one of his own.

"What if I want to buy something?"

"Your trial's coming up fast. Something tells me you won't be doing a lot of shopping over the next few years."

Cash stood up from behind the computer, and Aseem grabbed his upper arm, making sure Cash got a good look at the gun in his other hand. "Let's go. I'm going to walk you back to your scooter and make sure you get the hell out of here."

They shut the business center door and headed across the inn's grounds to the street where Cash had left the scooter. As they walked, Aseem maintained his cast-iron grip on Cash's arm.

"Go straight home, Cash. While you ride, think

about better ways to spend your remaining free time. Your obsession with Betty Snickerdoodle is not exactly healthy."

Cash started the scooter and repeatedly revved its modest engine to a high-pitched whine, sneering at Aseem, who couldn't stop snickering. Cash sputtered away on the dark country road as fast as the scooter could go, one middle finger aloft over his head.

Now that is what I call a good time, thought Aseem as he headed back towards his casita. Happily imagining telling Bea and Angela how he'd foiled Cash, he practically strutted down the driveway, no longer worried about the noise of gravel crunching beneath his feet.

As he passed the main entrance to the inn, he noticed the transom windows of the ballroom were no longer brightly lit. *Tournament must have ended a while ago now,* he thought. *Everyone will be waiting for me at the casita.* He picked up his pace and became focused on meeting up with the others, he didn't notice that two men who'd been lurking behind a car were now rushing towards him.

"Oof," he cried in pain as something hard struck the back of his head. He fell forward to the ground and then: lights out.

. . .

Crap! thought Foxy, watching the attack on Aseem from the shadows. He'd been tailing the two men as they prowled about the grounds. He was determined to figure out what kind of mischief they were up to—and he had to do it before breakfast, or else miss his chance.

Now, for some baffling reason, they'd paused their sneaking around to attack Aseem. What on earth was that about? Foxy had to decide whether to blow his own plan up in order to help Aseem or wait to see what these two did next.

He craned his neck for a better view, being cautious to avoid being seen. Were they attempting to move him? No—it seemed they were rolling him over. And were they taking something from his pocket?

Aseem lay still and the two sleazeballs slunk away. *Argh. I can't leave the kid there,* thought Foxy. *He might be seriously hurt.*

Foxy waited until he was sure he wouldn't be observed, then ran to Aseem's side. "Aseem, wake up. Can you hear me?"

Foxy shook Aseem's arm gently. Aseem groaned and opened his eyes, then touched the back of his head. A big lump was forming. His cheek was scraped up, too, from his hard fall onto the gravel. "Ouch."

"You OK?"

"I think so." With Foxy's help, he got back on his feet. His hoodie was unzipped, and when he patted his sides, he knew instantly what they'd taken.

"Did you see who attacked you?" Foxy said.

"No. I barely heard them. It all happened so fast."

"Let's get you back to your casita."

"I can get there on my own," Aseem protested. "I don't need you holding my arm."

"Just being cautious. You might have a concussion," Foxy said, loosening his grip. "I'll feel better if I make sure you get to your destination, at least."

Angela opened the door to the casita. Perry, Pat, and Bea were huddled around Aseem's desk on the other side of the room.

"Foxy, what are you doing? Why are you gripping him like that? Oh… oh my goodness, Aseem, what happened? What have you done, Foxy?!"

"It's not like that," Foxy said. "Someone attacked Aseem. I found him on the ground."

"Get out, Foxy!" Angela shrieked.

"It's OK, Angel," Aseem said. "He's telling the truth." Foxy released his arm, and Angela rushed to his side. She led him to his bed and sat next to him, examining the blood caked on the back of his head and on his cheek.

"So how is it you all are gathered here, anyway?" Foxy said. He was leaning on his right leg, trying to get a gander at the computer screen Perry, Pat, and Bea had been looking at.

"That's not really any of your business, is it?" Pat said, adopting an arms-akimbo superhero pose to more effectively block the screen. Like almost everyone else in the room, Pat had become irritated with Foxy's presumptuous prying.

Bea laughed at Foxy and cocked her head toward the clock on the nightstand. "You need your beauty rest, don't you, hot stuff? Wouldn't want you to miss the big reveal tomorrow!"

"Big reveal?"

"Oh, you know, the awards ceremony," said Bea. "I'm pretty sure you'll still want to see it, even though you didn't win anything."

Foxy scrutinized Bea's face until Angela interrupted him.

"Will you just *go,* Foxy? Why do you never leave when asked?"

Foxy sighed. *If only she hadn't spotted my gun,* he thought. He had to admire the tough side of Angela now on display, but he still liked her sweetness even more. He still held out hope that once all this was over, he'd have a shot with her.

"Aseem, if it wasn't Foxy who attacked you," Angela said once Foxy was gone, "then was it Cash?"

"It does seem like quite a coincidence that Foxy just happened to be wandering the grounds in the wee hours and ready to help you, just in time," snorted Bea. She didn't believe for a second that Foxy had anything to do with the attack on Aseem, but she was happy to help tarnish his image with Angela.

"It wasn't Foxy or Cash," said Aseem. "I had already watched Cash ride away. It was two guys who attacked me from behind, I'm almost sure."

"Do you remember anything else?" Angela said, still looking at him with concern, scanning for signs of further injury.

"A few things. Weird things," Aseem replied. "I'm sure I fell face-forward when I was hit on the head. I think that's how I scraped my cheek. But when Foxy woke me up, I was on my back. My hands were above my head, palms up. It was an awkward position. I'm certain I didn't fall that way. Plus, someone unzipped my hoodie—and they took something."

"Not Cash's phone!" exclaimed Bea. "Tell me you still have it."

"No, I've still got the phone," Aseem said, grinning as he took the phone out of his pocket to show Bea. "And I took care of everything we talked about. The plan went perfectly, Bea. But Perry, I'm sorry—your gun is gone."

"It's OK," said Perry. "That thing was a relic, anyway."

"I guess that rules Foxy out," Bea said. "Why would he need your gun? He's already got his own. I bet it's some kind of high-tech, money's-no-object automatic."

"So many guns! I'm the detective and it seems like I'm the only one who's not armed around here," said Pat. "I thought this was a classy event."

"Ask Angela," said Bea. "She invited these refined individuals into our home."

"I guess people aren't always what they seem," Angela said.

"At least you're finally learning, girlie."

CHAPTER 26

"You're amazing, Aseem," Angela said.

Angela, Bea, and Pat were in Aseem's room, listening to him explain the whole story of how he'd captured Cash and forced him to relinquish his troll blog, reviews, and phone. The monitor on his desk displayed the treasure trove of photos he'd downloaded from Cash's phone—including one showing a single guest sneaking out in the wee hours on the morning Eddie died. In the course of his obnoxious trespassing, Cash had inadvertently photographed a murder suspect.

"This might explain what happened to Eddie," said Angela. "It might even bring whoever harmed him to justice."

"Not to mention slamming the brakes on an

evil reviews troll!" exclaimed Bea. "Aseems's our hero, wouldn't you say, Angie? Best of all, I don't think he's done impressing us yet."

Angela didn't respond to Bea. She just walked across the room to Aseem and gave him a heartfelt hug. "Thank you."

"Sheesh," said Pat. "I came here to do detective training, but it's starting to feel like graduation day. Between Aseem's fantastic work with the phone, Angela's kitchen evidence, and your solving of the poker scam, Bea, maybe my work here is done."

"We couldn't have done it without you. And don't you get any ideas about closing down class early. I still need to learn all your computer tricks. Besides, when are you going to show me how to pick locks? I already told you how much I need that class."

"Wait, Bea's solved the poker scam? There's a poker scam?" said Angela.

"Shall we explain, Bea?" Perry said.

"We don't need to talk about it now, Angie," said Bea. "I'm going to spring my theory on everybody after the money's awarded tomorrow. It'll be a good show! But I want to get my hundred grand in my pocket before springing it on the perps that the jig is up!"

"Nice use of 'perps,'" said Pat, holding her hand up for a high five.

"So far we've got a suspicious-looking charity, a poker scam, poisonous doughnut ingredients, and possible murder," Angela said. "Bea, are you saying these things are all related somehow?"

"I think so—especially now that I've seen that photo of our potential murderer. But you've got to wait for my big ballroom scene, and I need another detail or two to confirm my theory."

Angela sighed. "OK. Tomorrow, then. But before we all turn in, Aseem and I should let McGregor know about our new evidence."

"If he asks, we'll tell him we found the phone after he left with Billy Ray's corpse, right, Bea?" said Pat, winking in Bea's direction.

"Do you think it was OK to let Cash have that belt buckle? It didn't occur to me it would be evidence," said Aseem, flipping through the photos on his computer.

"An act of mercy," said Bea. "Maybe he can trade it for ramen when things get rough in prison."

Finally, they hit "send" and their message was off to McGregor. Everyone said their goodnights and confirmed their plan for reconvening in the morning.

"I don't think you should stay here tonight, Aseem," Angela said. "You should stay with me. You might have a concussion. I don't think you should be alone."

Bea got a mischievous look in her eye and opened her mouth to speak. But she spotted Perry mouthing "be nice" toward her. She pouted, but stayed quiet. Perry chuckled silently and winked at her.

"I mean, what if those guys come after you again? They won't think to look for you in my suite. Besides, I've got a pull-out sofa," Angela added, looking straight at Bea with a glare that said *Get your mind out of the gutter*.

"What's with that look?" said Bea. "I think it's a good idea you and Aseem stick together. Just make sure you're not seen." Perry nodded at her approvingly. "Don't you two be late in the morning. I want everyone in position for my first big ballroom scene as wine country's new amateur detective."

Angela rolled her eyes, and Pat laughed. "Bea, you are aware that detectives don't typically assemble suspects in the ballroom, right?"

"Works for Hercule Poirot."

Pat bit her lip and gave up. "Angela, do you want me to walk back with you two?"

"No, it's best if we split up. Less chance of being spotted."

"Fair enough. Shall we, Bea? Perry, you coming, too?"

Pat, Bea, and Perry left. Angela and Aseem got ready to head back to her suite. "Maybe we should shut the drapes but leave a light on? To make it look like you might be here, in case your attackers try to find you?"

"Angel, I really appreciate it, but I don't think they're coming back. It's fine for me to stay here—"

"No arguments, please. You're coming with me. And don't worry, I'll sleep on the sofa. End of discussion."

In her suite, Angela told Aseem again that he should take the bed. "I'll be fine on the sofa. It's smaller and so am I. And I want to be able to keep an eye on you," she said with a smile. "Take off your hoodie and your shoes and get under the covers. You need rest. It's not long before we have to be back in the ballroom."

Aseem felt guilty—and a few other things as well—but was too exhausted to argue.

"I almost forgot," Angela said after ducking into the bathroom to change into flannel pajamas. "Would you like some aspirin?" She handed him a glass of water and doled two pills from a bottle into his hand.

Aseem took the painkillers gratefully, then climbed into bed. As soon as he was under the covers, fatigue took over and he began to drift off. Angela pulled the cushions off the loveseat. "Oh no," she said. "I guess it's not a pull-out."

Aseem pushed himself onto his elbows and looked at her. "Don't worry about it. I'm heading back to the casita. I'll be fine there."

"Nonsense!" said Angela, replacing the sofa cushions. "I'll just sleep on top of the sofa. She curled up into a ball on the little loveseat, which was far too short for her to lie flat.

"You won't get any sleep like that," Aseem said, sitting up and peeling back the covers. Angela hopped up and pulled the covers back over him.

"I've got an idea. It's a big bed. You stay under the covers, and I'll sleep on the other half, on top of them. Perfectly respectable."

"You'll freeze."

"I won't. I'm wearing flannel pajamas. And I've got an extra blanket. If that's not enough, maybe you and I can share the top comforter."

Too tired to argue, Aseem agreed. But once Angela was lying beside him, he found the urge to sleep fading away. She wanted to talk, too. She rolled onto her side to face him.

"Fancy meeting you here," Angela said, smiling.

Aseem rolled onto his side and looked at her. "Come here often?"

Angela giggled. "Did you ever think we'd end up in bed together?"

"Technically, you're not in bed—you're not under the covers."

"Just answer the question."

"I plead the fifth."

"Don't forget, I'm your boss," Angela said playfully. "I could insist that you answer."

"See? That's the problem. Even if I did think so… you shouldn't even ask me these kinds of questions."

Angela looked at him seriously. He was right. She should think about the bigger picture. She felt sad and flustered. Another rookie mistake. She wasn't getting off to a great start as company president. Every day, it seemed, brought another harsh reminder of how much she had to learn.

Aseem saw how disappointed she looked and felt a pang. All this time, he'd wondered how she felt. Now he knew, but… timing. He sighed and caressed her cheek. "I guess there's only one solution," he said, grinning. "You're going to have to fire me."

"That's a problem, because I can't run this place without you—and I wouldn't dare try," she said with a melancholy smile. "Would it make a difference if you were an independent contractor?"

Aseem laughed. "I don't know, Angel. That sounds like a legal matter. Maybe we should try to get some sleep and figure it out in the morning. The sun's coming up in just a couple of hours."

WALTER AND JAMES maneuvered the loaded dolly down the patio stairs as quietly as possible. At least the plan—the crazy, new, unplanned plan—was so far going without a hitch.

"Your brother finally had one good idea about unlocking the French door," whispered Walter.

"Drapes being shut didn't hurt."

"Unfortunately, it's his fault we needed Plan B. Mr. Subtle with the chip stacks. And your idea of attacking Aseem was just as bad! What is the matter with you two?" Walter was spitting as he whispered, his rage over the botched arrangement overwhelming his desperation not to be heard.

"Are you bound and determined to wreck a good thing?"

"I wasn't sure how your idea would work," James whispered back. "I just don't see how we could have pulled it off with Aseem without knocking him out."

"People can die from head injuries like that. We're not in some Hollywood movie. If there's anything we don't need, it's another dead body."

"At least we got what we needed, right? Besides, none of it matters as long as we don't get caught. Let's keep our heads down, focus, and get out of here while we still can."

"The others better have the car ready."

They put the dolly down on the grass that ran alongside the driveway, hoping to wheel it along without crunching on the gravel. The security lights illuminating the exterior of the building worried Walter. "Let's try to cross the driveway as quickly and quietly as we can, to get out of the light. Take off your shoes."

They put their shoes on top of their cargo, then picked up the dolly from the bottom. Both of them groaned softly with the effort. "Make it quick," said Walter. "My feet are freezing." A minute later, they placed the dolly on the grass on the other side of the drive.

"Better," said Walter. The two men put their shoes on and wheeled the dolly off the grass to the street. The others had moved the big black SUV there earlier in the day, parking it on the other side of the street, far from the nearest light pole. They hurried across the street toward the open back door of the vehicle.

"We could use help lifting this thing into the back," Walter hissed to the passengers. Together, the men hoisted the heavy object into the back. "Keep it face-side up," grunted James.

"Where to now?" said the driver. "It's not like we can get that thing onto a plane."

"I'll climb in the back and figure that out as we drive," said James. "Lee, you just focus on getting us on our way to the airport."

Angela and Aseem had each managed about an hour of fitful sleep when both were awake once more, both wanting to talk, neither knowing what to say. Faint light was seeping through the gap in the drapes. The sun was almost up.

Aseem broke the silence, shifting onto his side to face her. "Angel, you asked if I thought we'd end up here—if we'd have ended up here the normal way. Of course, I hoped so. You're beautiful and loyal and determined and so, so smart. I think you were always my dream girl, even if I didn't always realize it. But now you're making your own dreams happen. The last thing I'd ever want to do is interfere—"

"Shh," Angela said, placing a finger on his lips. "You should have stopped at 'dream girl.'" She turned to face him, smiling now. She leaned in to kiss him.

Their lips about to touch, Aseem wanted to resist. "Too… complicated…." But his hand on the nape of her neck said something different.

The light on the internet device in the corner of Angela's room began to flash, and the familiar boop-boop-boop tone demanded attention. Aseem and Angela leaned back and looked at each other with wry smiles: the moment lost, the dilemma seemingly resolved.

"Jackson calling," announced the device.

"Ms. Garcia? I mean, Angela? I hope I'm not waking you."

"No worries, Jackson," Angela said with a sigh. "I was awake."

"The servers were setting up the breakfast area in the ballroom for the presentation this morning. And, well, there's a pretty big problem. I thought you'd want to look into it before people start showing up. It looks like some things... have been tampered with. It seems like someone broke into our supply closet, too."

"OK, I'll get dressed and head down right now. Will you tell Bea?"

"Yes, I'll call her next. Do you know if Aseem's still staying in the casita? There's a tech issue, too, and he's not answering the call there."

"Oh, yes, he's—um, maybe try his cell?" said Angela, winking at Aseem.

A moment later, Aseem pulled his ringing cell from his hoodie pocket. "Thanks, Jackson, I'll be down to check it out right away."

Angela brought a change of clothes into the bathroom and emerged a few minutes later looking miraculously refreshed. Her thick, glossy hair was tied up in a loose bun on top of her head and her face was lightly made up.

She put the aspirin bottle and a fresh glass of water on the desk for Aseem, who was typing into his phone. "Give me a minute. There's one problem I can take care of remotely. There, it's done." He slugged three aspirin, chasing them with the water. "Thank you. My head started throbbing again once I stood up."

"I thought it might," Angela said. "Unfortunately, what you really need is rest. Do you want to freshen up before we head to the ballroom?"

"I think I'll head back to the casita. That fix I just did bought a few minutes to shower and change. I'll see you down in the ballroom."

CHAPTER 27

"Well, that's not at all what I expected," laughed Bea.

"Icing on the cake of this horrible project," Angela said. "On the plus side, I'm almost too tired to try to figure out what screwup of mine led to this disaster."

The two women stood by the open door of the control room. A black cloth had been tossed over the camera above the door, and its wires had been cut. Inside the room, there was a large, empty space where the big safe previously stood.

"Buck up, girlie!" said Bea. "You can't blame yourself because there are bad people in the world. Besides, Perry or I should have thought to bolt the safe down. Can't pin that one on you."

"I can when you warned me that this stupid event had the smell of scam. You were exactly right. Don't you suppose this latest unseemly incident fits right in with the sleazy poker, dubious charity, and poisoning of Eddie?"

"Well, when you put it that way," said Bea, still snickering.

"How can you laugh at a time like this? This was your moment to celebrate your tournament victory, along with the other two winners. Now we have to tell them—somehow—all the money is gone. Two dead, $500,000 missing. I don't think insurance will even cover any of it. I wonder if we'll ever be able to get insurance in the future." Angela covered her eyes with her hands.

"Don't you worry, girlie. Trust me, this is not ideal, but it's not going to ruin everything—not by a longshot," said Bea. "Have you called Officer Lackadaisical?"

"Jackson called McGregor as soon as he saw we'd had a break-in. He was already coming over to collect our evidence for Eddie's case, anyway."

"Maybe now he'll move a little quicker. Is Aseem on his way here?"

As if on cue, Aseem joined them and assessed the damage for himself. He looked at the open control room with wide eyes and a wry smile. "I bet a few people are skipping breakfast."

"That'll make it easier to confirm who the crooks are," laughed Bea. "I just hope it doesn't take the fizz out of my presentation."

The main ballroom doors weren't yet open. Only employees were supposed to have access, to finish preparing for the award breakfast. But Foxy had managed to maneuver his way through, skating in behind the servers who were putting finishing touches on the festive coffee and pastry set-up.

"You're a little early, Foxtrot," said Bea. "We're not starting for another 15 minutes."

Foxy blew right past her, ignoring her comment. He'd spotted the damaged camera and the open control room door and charged in to have a look.

"Sorry, Bea," said Pat, hustling into the ballroom after Foxy. "I tried to stop him, but he wasn't having any of it." The twins and their glamorous companions followed him into the room.

"What a shock," said Bea. "Foxy's sticking his nose in."

Foxy emerged from the control room with a stern expression. "It's my job to be nosy." He reached into his pocket and pulled out what looked like his wallet. He flipped it open and revealed an FBI ID.

The twins' stunning girlfriends gazed at Foxy. In unison, their slender arms slid slowly off the shoulders of their identical Ken-doll boyfriends, and the beginnings of smiles surfaced on their flawless, blank faces.

"Some chicks just can't resist a secret agent man," whined Pat. "Nobody even seems to notice when I whip out my private eye ID."

"I was kind of hoping you were in on it, Foxy, but at the end of the day, I couldn't make the pieces fit, especially once you had that tête-à-tête with McGregor beside Billy Ray's body," said Bea with a sigh. "Either the two of you had to be cops, or the two of you were crooks. McGregor doesn't seem like he's got enough energy to pull off a double life, so I had to guess cop. Sorry, Angela. I hate to admit it, but Foxy is not so bad after all."

"I'm confused to say the least," said Angela.

Foxy ignored the women and pulled on a thin latex glove he'd drawn from his pocket. He carefully moved the door of the control room so he could look behind it. He noticed a bit of paper and picked it up with a pair of tweezers, tucking it into a plastic bag he'd also brought with him.

"They got in and out through here," yelled

Aseem from across the expansive room. He'd pulled back the drape on one of the French doors and discovered that the lock had been jammed. "I guess they came back in through the patio after we locked the main ballroom doors for the night and brought the safe out the same way."

"That safe was awful heavy, though," said Pat. "Even if a couple of guys were carrying it, still not easy to do quietly."

"Maybe that explains something weird Jackson told me," Angela said. "He said it looked like someone had been in the supply closet. The dolly was missing."

"Don't touch anything else!" barked Foxy. "It's all evidence now." He ran past Aseem out through the patio door. He quickly scanned the area for any clues, then ran back into the ballroom.

"Aseem, I suppose that video camera's a brick now, right? What about the recording? Is there any way to determine when the safe went missing? I wonder how they got into the control room. No signs of force or damage on the door."

"He could tell you who took it, Foxy, if you'd just slow down a sec," Bea said. "We promised to wait for McGregor before presenting our evidence."

"What? If you have evidence, you get ready to

present it now," said Foxy. "Waiting is not an option."

"Oh, boy, it's just like what I've heard about you fibbies!" Bea said, rubbing her hands with delight. "Shame you can't just share credit with locals. Can't you all just get along?"

"What are you talking about? McGregor knows all about my case. He welcomes my help. Queue up your 'presentation,' Bea. I mean it. I need to step out to make a call, but I'll be back in a minute and expect you to be ready to share what you've got."

Foxy pulled his fancy phone out of his pocket and punched a number as he moved toward the exit. He began barking instructions involving a helicopter, alerts to local police, and calls to area airports. A far cry from the smooth operator of the past three nights, this Foxy was a forceful man of action.

"We're not cutting our local Officer Friendly out of a big collar," Bea hollered sweetly after him. "Be patient, and we won't just tell you who took the safe. Aseem will show you exactly where they are."

Foxy abruptly disconnected his call, then turned around and walked back to Bea, glowering. He looked down into her eyes as if staring down a vicious street thug, not a 90-pound morsel of a woman he could pick up with one hand.

"Listen, you wily little cardsharp," said Foxy. "Your cagey routine is all well and fine for the poker table. But we're talking dangerous felons here. And we're not on some TV show!"

"Just cool your jets, handsome," Bea said, stepping back. She wasn't inclined to mess with law enforcement. In fact, she'd learned years ago that smart gamblers stayed on the right side of the law. But it was hard for her not to be stubborn, since she hated being bossed around more than almost anything.

"Quit fooling around, Bea! If you have information about this case, spill it—now. Otherwise, you're withholding evidence. And you're bringing Aseem down with you, too. How'd you both like to end up under arrest?"

Aseem looked panicked and started to respond, but Angela beat him to it. "So, you're really FBI, Foxy?" said Angela gently. Foxy rolled his eyes and showed his badge again. "Yes!"

"Bea, I know we promised McGregor, but I think we have to do as Foxy says. What if the culprits get away? It's not just the money. We're thinking one of them murdered Eddie, right?"

Bea frowned. “OK, OK. I see your point. Aseem, show him.”

Aseem vaulted up the steps onto the stage beside the control room. He pulled back the garland he’d draped on the gigantic LED screen a few days before and found a remote attached to the back with a bit of Velcro. He tapped the remote. The display started up, and a browser launched.

“I attached a GPS tracker to the safe. When Jackson told me about the break-in, I turned it on. Now we can watch where the safe goes online.” A map appeared on the screen. A blip was moving along the 505 freeway. “Interesting route. Maybe they want to find a country spot where they can bust the safe open. It’s not like they can carry it on an airplane.”

Aseem paused for a minute to text Foxy the URL and the password.

“Good job, Aseem,” said Bea. “Don’t you think he’s awfully clever, Angie? Definitely more than just a pretty face.”

“Of course I know he’s awfully clever, Bea,” said Angela, rolling her eyes. “Why do you think I hired him?”

“Excellent work, Aseem. They’re in for a big surprise,” Foxy said, tapping quickly on his phone, springing into action once more.

"You have no idea," cracked Bea. "Wait 'til they open the safe!"

"Angela, please tell Jackson I need access to all guest suites. I need to start combing this entire building for evidence. The grounds, too. I'm going to call for some help. And nobody leaves until I say so!"

Foxy rushed out of the ballroom to begin his search, phone to his ear, almost colliding with a sheepish, slightly winded Officer McGregor.

"What did I miss? I heard over the radio that the FBI has dispatched a helicopter near here. That can't be related to anything happening here, though, right?" He was quick to add the last bit, looking clumsily over his shoulder to be sure Foxy was out of earshot.

"Don't worry about it," Pat said. "Foxy dropped his cover. He's thrown you under the bus, too. No collar for you!"

"Who cares about that? As far as I'm concerned, they can handle it," said McGregor with a shrug.

"I, for one, feel protected and served," snarked Bea. "Just kidding. You're smart not to get all territorial. What matters is solving the crime. Speaking of which, your timing is perfect. Now that Foxy's gone, we can restart my big reveal. Aseem, can we start over?

"Shame our other pals can't be here," Bea snickered. "I was looking forward to seeing their faces! Too bad, but I'm still getting my big ballroom scene. Aseem, maybe we should dim the lights a bit? Grab a pastry and take a seat, everybody!"

CHAPTER 28

Bea was holding court in the ballroom. Perry had joined the group, but the audience for her big moment was sparse. Lee, Harry, Walter, James, Frank, and Foxy were all missing, leaving nearly half the chairs empty—and the chairs they'd set out only covered a small fraction of the ballroom's large footprint. Bea's audience was just Rex and Max, their girlfriends, Pat, Perry, Aseem, Angela, and Officer McGregor. Nothing could dampen Bea's enthusiasm, though. Her posture inexplicably straight as a rod, she seemed to have gained an inch or two of height, and was strutting across the stage using her cane to point at the big screen.

"Perry, I'm glad you're here, since it was the

cheating you and I spotted that really got my investigation going in a big way," Bea said pompously. Officer McGregor looked confused. Angela tipped her chin down and covered her mouth with her hand, suppressing a giggle. "That work we did together was crucial to cracking the case. Bravo."

Perry nodded solemnly.

Bea then proceeded to explain how she and Perry detected cheating at the tables. "Right away, on the first night, we noticed betting patterns that helped one player chip up fast. And it seemed like certain stacks grew during the breaks—like someone had a supply of extra chips and was adding them to those stacks. At first I thought it was my imagination, but then Perry and I decided to look at the video footage."

Rex and Max looked at each other anxiously.

"Don't worry, you two," Bea said, laughing. "Nobody ever suspected you. It wasn't any of us three, it wasn't Foxy, and it wasn't either of the two dead guys."

"The cheaters just happen to be the people who skipped out last night," Pat chimed in supportively. "Quite a co-inky-dink!"

"That's correct, Pat," said Bea with a forced smile. "But I must ask you to hold your comments until the end of the presentation. There will be time for audience questions at the end."

Bea continued, explaining that another clue was the failure of the video set-up. "By the second night, I was sure someone had interfered with the video. After all, we knew it was set up right. Aseem here is a technology genius." As she mentioned Aseem's name, she waved her hand in his direction in the manner of a game show model. Then she stared at Angela to be sure she was paying attention.

"Once the second night's video was lost, Aseem came up with the brilliant idea of the second camera—the one attached to this video screen, which no one else knew about. It captured exactly who stole the safe.

"But I'm getting ahead of myself. Because long before we got to the second night of missing video, we already suspected a scam was afoot—a big one!"

Bea paused for a moment for dramatic effect. She took a few contemplative paces around her cane, then turned back to her audience.

"From the moment you all arrived, there were clues. Everything about the tournaments seemed rigged. Perry spotted trouble right away. The bag of cash Lee stored in the safe—the total of our

$50,000 apiece buy-ins—looked off. She had wrapped the stacks and taped them up into bricks, so we couldn't count it. She said she was keeping things under tight control. But Perry took one look at the sack of bricks and was sure it didn't total up to the $500K total of our ten buy-ins. He thought they contained about half that amount. Naturally, he would spot the difference, since he runs a casino for his day job."

A few of the people in Bea's little audience gasped. "That's right," she continued. "It looked darn fishy right from the get-go. But we couldn't be sure there wasn't an honest explanation. Maybe one or two of the players had wired her the money, and Lee decided she didn't need to bring it here as cash. Or perhaps she'd told one of her long-time players they could pay another way—say, with bitcoins. Unorthodox, questionable, for sure—but, hey, not much about this tournament is normal. I'm sure it's obvious now, though," Bea said, tilting her head toward the open control room door, "Lee was planning to rip us paying players off from the start.

"Perry and I figured, if it turned out some buy-ins really were missing, then some players had to be counting on winning without anteing up. Because that's the only way they'd never have to put any money in—if they knew for sure they'd win. Hence," she said, pausing and raising her index finger for dramatic effect, "the coordinated cheating. And hence the benefit of getting the best player at the table, Eddie, out of the game."

"But Bea," interjected Angela, "weren't you the best player at the table?"

"Very flattering, Angela. I doubt that's true," Bea said with false modesty. "Even if it were true, they had no way of knowing it. Eddie was the player they thought they had to worry about. They'd all heard he was training for the World Series of Poker. And he was proving their fears right by dominating the first night's game."

Aseem then clicked to a slide of the website Angela found, which showed the warning about the ingredients in the flour. "As you can see," continued Bea, "this would not be a good choice of flour to keep Eddie safe. More like the opposite."

"So it may have been intentional on Lee's part—not accidental," Angela added.

"Yes. Didn't she make a point of insisting the flour be used for a snack during the first night's tournament? Perhaps she was only planning to bump Eddie from the tournament, not bump him off entirely, though," Bea said, cackling inappropriately.

"I'd like a copy of that screenshot and the link," piped up Officer McGregor. "Brilliant find, Angela."

"At the start of day two, we learn that Eddie died. Did someone murder him? Or did he die of a complication of the first reaction—Angie, what's that called again?"

"You mean a biphasic reaction? That's a secondary attack related to the first one, with no additional exposure," Angela said. "That's what the doctors thought happened, at least at first."

"But my peeps in the hospital thought different! They thought someone deliberately exposed Eddie again!" blurted Pat. "Shoot, I'm sorry, Bea. I couldn't help myself."

"That's OK, Pat. That information from your peeps—combined with a little luck—got us on the trail of a murderer!" Bea said, adopting a deep, melodramatic tone. "Someone might have gone to finish Eddie off—but who? Aseem, it's time to show everyone the face of our suspect."

"Is that… Walter?" said Rex.

"Indeed," said Bea, looking at Officer McGregor. "His last name is Wells. Walter Wells. At least that's what he said his name was. We had a hard time finding anyone matching his name and description online. Whoever he is, that picture shows him leaving the inn before dawn on the morning Eddie died."

"Huh. He seemed like a nice enough guy," said Max.

"Foxy's got Aseem's tracker and the FBI is now on the chase, Officer McGregor," said Angela. "But is there anything else we need to do to be sure he doesn't escape?"

"The FBI will have put all local police on alert. They'll take care of apprehending the suspect. I'll do my part by gathering all the evidence you have to offer," replied McGregor, settling back down in his chair with a second coffee and pastry.

Bea smirked. "Yes, let us continue to do our fair share. Aseem, why don't you show the slide showing the connecting suites?

"Aseem helped us look at the card key log, which showed no one had reentered their room before breakfast that morning. We thought that meant no one left here for Eddie's hospital room. But then I had the brainstorm that broke the case wide open!" said Bea.

"The secret was the adjoining rooms. Any one of these three—Foxy, Walter, and James—would have access to his room without a key, as long as a neighbor was there to let him in. To figure out which guy went out that night, we had to get a little lucky."

Bea went on to explain how she and Pat found Cash's phone and his photos while looking for their reviews troll. "Billy Ray's annoyance with that nasty blog inadvertently helped us find the most important piece of evidence."

Officer McGregor stood up. "Bea, amazing work. I've seen all I need to see. Aseem, I assume you'll be sending me a copy of all of your video and these slides? Angela, will you help me with the rest of the evidence?"

"Of course," said Angela.

"Amazing work?" said Bea. "Aren't you going to tell me to keep my nose out of police work in the future? To leave the detecting to detectives?"

"Listen, we're shorthanded around here. And it's not like we get a lot of violent crimes in wine country. In the future, if you want to help us find stolen grapes or solve our lost pet cases, knock yourself out," McGregor said absently, surveying the remaining pastries. "Mind if I take these to go?" He bundled a mix of croissants and scones into a napkin and headed out the door.

"I hope he thinks to show Walter's picture to the smoothie place near the hospital," Pat said. "There might be a witness there. Maybe even a record of what he bought. Heck, maybe even video."

"I'll suggest it when I pass the other evidence along," said Angela.

Rex, Max, and their twin companions got up from their seats and started making their way to the door, too. As they prepared to leave, Connie and Bijou walked in. "Is it OK if I just grab some coffee? I was hoping it would be OK, even though I'm not really part of the group." She looked tired, and her eyes were puffy from crying.

"Of course it's OK. And of course you're part of the group," said Angela, putting her arm around Connie's shoulders to welcome her, then reaching down to pet her canine friend.

"I'm very glad you're here, Connie. I'm glad you're all here. Rex, Max, ladies, please sit back down for just one more moment. Because I haven't even gotten to the best part!" said Bea triumphantly. "Aseem, you ready?"

With a loud clunk, Aseem unhooked a metal fastener behind the right edge of the enormous display. As he pulled that side of the monitor away from the wall, the massive hinges that held it, invisible from the front, squeaked in protest. After a few moments of tugging, Aseem revealed what was hiding behind the hefty display: a second, smaller safe.

After a few clicks on the number pad, a scan of his retina, and a press of his fingerprint, Aseem was able to open the safe, revealing its amazing contents: a canvas sack just like the one in the stolen safe, filled with several brick-like packages, each heavily wrapped in plastic and layers and layers of tape.

"And that, my friends, is the best news of the day: That's our money! And we're going to roll back the clock, pretend the tournament never happened, and take all of it back. Well, most of it, anyway."

Rex, Max, and Connie's mouths were agape. Beaming with pride, Bea explained how the money hadn't spent a single night in the safe their crooked opponents had stolen.

"Once Perry noticed the cash was off, we thought we'd better keep our money safe. So we made up a decoy bag and stuck it in the big safe and put the real money in this one. When the videos started failing, we were sure we'd done the right thing. No one was the wiser. Thanks to Aseem, the screen that was showing our Yule log was hiding our money the whole time!

"Now we've got some decisions to make," said

Bea. "$5,000 of what we each paid in was for Lee's charity. But I think it's safe to say that must be a scam, am I right, Angela?"

"Yes, Bea," said Angela, with a sigh. "You were right all along." Angela then explained that she'd looked into the charity's tax filings. With the help of some basic accounting tips from the internet, she'd been able to determine easily that the charity was a sham.

"Naturally, it's terrible news that Lee has been ripping people off in the name of charity," said Bea. "But at least she's not getting away with it this time. My proposition to the three of you is that we take the charity money and donate it to a real cause. Lee said you all used to have your holiday event in Paradise. How about we donate to one of the organizations helping those poor folks whose homes burned down?"

"I think that's a great idea," said Connie. "In fact, I don't want a refund of Billy Ray's buy-in, either. Donate it all to help those people in Paradise."

Rex and Max said they'd like to do the same.

"Fantastic!" said Bea. "I'll do the same with my money, too. Now there's one bit of accounting—our fees for rentals and staffing of the inn were also coming out of our buy-ins. But Angela, I think we can agree to do the event at cost, and donate our profit. What do you think?"

"I love that plan," said Angela. "And tomorrow is Christmas. What a perfect way to celebrate it."

Bea stepped down from the stage while Aseem locked the cash back up. Hugs and handshakes were exchanged, as Bea and Angela thanked Rex, Max, and Connie for their generosity.

"All things considered, Angela, we really enjoyed our stay at your inn," said Rex.

"We were thinking we'd like to host a chic little holiday party of our own here next year. With plenty of time to plan, we're sure you'd come up with something even more spectacular," added Max.

"That's very flattering. Thank you," said Angela. "But I think we'll stick with our mission of hosting Betty Snickerdoodle's fans from now on. I'm sure you agree, don't you, Bea?"

CHAPTER 29

"I'm so grateful. And so impressed." Angela was standing next to Aseem as he stood near the top of the stepladder, taking down the damaged camera outside the control room.

"Don't be too impressed," Aseem said with a laugh. "I never did figure out how those jerks foiled this camera's recordings."

"That reminds me. You never showed us how the thieves broke into the control room. Was that captured on your other video?"

"Not really. The video shows Walter and James going in with the dolly and backing out with the safe on it. But they got inside in nothing flat, and the door wasn't damaged. Honestly, I'm stumped."

"I suppose it doesn't matter, since the safe was a decoy, anyway."

"That was a stroke of genius by Bea and Perry, no doubt."

"I don't have to tell you how much Bea loves outsmarting jerks like that."

"Yeah. It's contagious!" Aseem chuckled. His head was starting to feel a little better, and he was able to enjoy the memory of his own role in putting Cash in his place and helping bring down the poker crooks.

The two of them worked together to take down the fancy decorations they'd put up around the ballroom, replacing them with the more homespun ones Angela had originally selected to create the feel of Betty Snickerdoodle's wine-country home.

"It's a relief to put these three days behind us," Angela said. "Lessons were learned. I suspect I've got plenty more ahead of me."

Aseem had moved the stepladder beside the French doors, near the corner where he'd hung the mistletoe. He was standing on the second rung of the ladder, reaching up to take down the pretty green ball of leaves.

"Wait—leave it," Angela said impulsively, as she moved beside the ladder and touched Aseem's knee. He paused for a moment and stepped off the ladder.

"Angel," he said, placing his hands on her shoulders and looking into her eyes. "I want you to trust me, because I've thought about this a lot. I want to be part of your success."

"That's what I want, too," Angela said. "So why do I think there's a 'but' coming?"

"The time is now for everything you have planned for the inn and your grand vision for Betty, Inc. Let me help you bring it to life. I want to—but you have to agree, that will mean the timing's not right for us—except for working together. It's hard enough to build a business without complicating things right out of the gate."

"I guess this is what they mean about not having it all," Angela said, eyes downcast to hide the tears that were starting to well up.

"I have no doubt you'll have everything you want eventually," Aseem said, with a soft laugh. He felt relieved. Once he'd said the words aloud, he felt certain he was doing the right thing.

Angela hugged him and kissed him on the cheek. "I hope it's still OK for me to hug you."

"Of course it is. We're still friends—even if you are my boss. Merry Christmas, Angel," said Aseem.

"If this is my present, I'm not sure I like it," Angela said. "But Merry Christmas to you, too, my dear friend."

~

THE INTERNET TUBE in Bea's suite lit up and its boop tones sounded. Bea and Pat were in the middle of discussing the plan for the night—for their Christmas Eve celebration. Angela had invited both of them to her mom's house in Sacramento for dinner and holiday cheer, and they were very much looking forward to it.

"Kitchen calling," said the tube's sweet voice.

"Bea, can you come to the kitchen as soon as possible?" Angela said. "There's something I want to show you. Bring Pat, too."

"Yes, boss lady!" cracked Bea, slapping her knee. "I love saying that."

"But I'm not your boss. You're the CEO and I'm the president, remember? Anyway, make your way to the kitchen as soon as you can. No need to change or anything."

The tube disconnected and Bea snorted with laughter. "I can't believe she thought I would change this fantastic outfit. I don't think I've ever looked better! Maybe she was thinking I'd dress down a bit."

"Ready to go, then?" Pat said. "I'm so glad not to have to wear that stiff security guard outfit anymore. I have to admit, it was a little unflattering." She was back in her plaid flannel shirt and a loose pair of chinos.

As the two of them walked past the lobby toward the kitchen, the last of the golden late-afternoon light streamed in through the main doors. It provided a beautiful halo effect for the tinkling decorations in the deserted lobby. Jackson, and all the other staff, had left for the holiday—their pockets and bank accounts bulging with unexpected bonuses from Bea and Angela, plus generous tips from Connie and the twins.

Just as in the ballroom, Angela had restored the warm and homey Betty Snickerdoodle-style decorations in the lobby. The big tree was covered in lights and handcrafted ornaments. Sweet Santas, elves, candy canes, and stockings galore adorned the walls and shelves. The room radiated family, love, and glad tidings.

"You gotta admit, Betty's world is pretty corny," laughed Bea. "But don't you just love it?"

"Hey, do you smell something delicious? I sure do!" said Pat.

As they walked through the swinging doors, the tantalizing scents grew stronger—and their source was revealed. Angela's mother was cooking away in the inn's large, gleaming kitchen. Angela and Connie were there, too, sipping hot drinks in clear mugs, the cinnamon sticks in each contributing to the festive fragrance in the room.

"Surprise!" said Angela. "My mom thought it would be more fun to cook in this big kitchen. Since Connie was here, I thought we could make a party of it. I called Perry—he'll be over later, too."

Maria hugged Bea and Pat, then turned her attention back to her work. She opened one oven to check on a glorious pork roast, its irresistible aroma filling the room. "Needs about an hour more. Just enough time for appetizers. Will you help yourselves to mulled wine or cider?"

"I recommend the mulled wine. We are in Napa Valley, after all," said Connie. "And it's absolutely delicious."

"Connie and I have started working on dessert," said Angela. "By 'working,' I mean decorating the gingerbread men that my mother already rolled and cut for us. Later, I'll demonstrate even greater expertise by taking my mother's famous flan out of the refrigerator."

"Shall we set the table?" Connie asked.

"Yes, please. Angela and I pushed two tables together in the ballroom for us," said Maria. "I just need to set the vegetables to cook. Then I'll bring the appetizers out for us all to snack on. I hope everyone's hungry."

The four of them set the large table with a red tablecloth and pretty plates stenciled with holly leaves. Angela placed Christmas-themed platters and serving utensils onto the spare table, and Pat and Connie carried the two punch bowls into the ballroom and placed them on the bar. The finishing touch was a lovely centerpiece of holly and candles.

"Hey girlie, what about the Yule log?" Bea asked.

"Great idea," Angela said, hopping onto the stage and turning on the display.

"I love your outfit, Angela," said Connie. "Is that sweater from the Betty Snickerdoodle collection?"

"Indeed it is!" Angela was wearing cream-colored jeans, tall boots, and an off-white sweater with fluffy faux fur trim and a delicate reindeer applique design. Her hair was tied back in a swingy high ponytail.

"I'm surprised you haven't mentioned my outfit yet," said Bea. "I thought for sure you'd say something at the presentation this morning. My sweater's from the gift collection, too!"

"The sweater is great, Bea," said Angela, maintaining her focus on just that one garment. The pretty merino-wool sweater Bea had chosen had a lovely Christmas tree pattern. But it was not well-complemented by the bright red and green argyle leggings she wore with it.

"I see you're looking at my bottoms," Bea cackled. "It's a little hard to appreciate at first. But chic people these days avoid too much matchy-matchy. Kind of surprised you didn't know that, Angie."

"Learn something every day," said Angela, biting her lip to keep from laughing.

Maria saved the moment by wheeling in a beautiful tray filled with a mix of Mexican and American holiday snacks: tiny tamales, shrimp cocktail, pumpkin empanadas, pigs in blankets, and more.

"It's beautiful," said Connie, tears in her eyes. "This is so much fun. Thank you so much for including me."

"Thank you for being here," said Angela.

"I've got news," said Pat after taking a bite of a pumpkin empanada and *ooh*ing and *aah*ing over it. "I spoke to Foxy a little while ago. They managed to capture the five rascals on their way to the airport. They're all spending Christmas Eve in jail."

"Yay!" said Bea, Angela, and Connie all at once.

"He shared a couple of other interesting tidbits—professional detective type stuff." Pat cocked her head and assumed a pedantic tone as she began to explain what Foxy had told her. She appeared to have picked up some stylistic tricks from Bea's big reveal. "I couldn't help but be curious about the case. Truth is, I've never worked on a felony before, let alone a murder. And it turns out Lee and her gang might have murdered some of the other players who mysteriously died during some of their previous tournaments!"

The other ladies gasped all at once.

"Foxy said he's been working on the case, tracking Lee, Harry, and the rest of the gang for almost two years. He's really happy it's resolved, but regrets he couldn't stop poor Eddie's death."

"Did he say how they broke into the control room?" asked Angela. "Aseem was wondering, too."

"The forensics team is still working on it. Foxy found some paper by the door that looks like a clue. They defeated the fingerprint scanner somehow—the paper might be part of the answer. Funny, he mentioned that he'd share more about it when he sees you next month, Angela. So… I guess that means you've got a date?"

Angela turned a familiar shade of pink. "Just coffee. Why would I refuse?" She spotted Bea's grumpy expression, but interrupted her before she could say what Angela knew she was about to say. "Bea, just for the record, Aseem and I are dear friends, and that's how it's going to stay—we talked about it, by the way."

"Does that mean you have to go running after the first hot guy who comes your way?"

"It's just *coffee,* Bea. I'm not getting married. I don't even know if it's a date. Besides, didn't you admit that Foxy is one of the good guys?"

Bea frowned and shrugged, at a loss for words for once.

"How about a toast?" said Pat. "Grab a drink, girls." The ladies each picked up a mug with their beverage of choice. They clinked their glasses and heartily wished each other merry Christmas.

"It was a challenging few days," said Angela. "But it all worked out in the end." But as she said it, she realized that things hadn't worked out for Billy Ray in the end, and she looked at Connie with embarrassment. "I'm sorry, Connie. That was insensitive."

"It's OK, Angela," Connie said. "I'm sad for

Billy Ray. But the truth is... maybe not sad for me. Billy Ray wasn't right for me. I don't think I would have done anything about it, though, if he were still alive."

"To new beginnings," announced Bea, raising her glass again. "And the New Year around the corner."

"Hear, hear!" said the ladies.

"Since we're talking about new beginnings, there's something I'd like to share," Connie said. Her face was pink, her smile brighter than it had been since she arrived at the inn. She looked just a little bolder, too—perhaps it was the warm wine, or maybe just the mildly intoxicating notion of a fresh start.

"I've been a fan of yours, Bea—or, should I say, a fan of Betty's—for ages. For years now, I've even dreamed about trying my hand at writing stories like yours. You've been such an inspiration. And so the thing is—" she said, stopping to take a deep breath, "I've given it a shot! I've written a novella. And I was wondering—feel free to say no, of course—but I was wondering if you'd be willing to read it."

Before Bea could answer—perhaps afraid of what her answer would be—Angela piped up.

"That's wonderful news, Connie. Of course, we'll both read it. Isn't that right, Bea?"

"Of course we both will," said Bea. "Why don't you come back next month for BettyCon? You could take my writing seminar."

"Your writing seminar?" Angela said with a gulp.

"Didn't I tell you about it, Angie? Great idea, right?"

"I hadn't even considered BettyCon," said Connie. "Billy Ray wouldn't have wanted to go, and that would have meant I couldn't, either."

"Not a bad way to start a new year," said Angela.

"You might even get a new career out of it!" Bea said.

LATER THAT NIGHT, stuffed to the gills with delicious food, Angela, Bea, and Pat were clearing plates and cleaning up the kitchen. Maria was taking a much-deserved nap in her suite, and Connie had taken a snack of leftovers back to Bijou.

"I guess I'm glad to hear about the writing seminar, Bea," Angela said, breaking the silence. "All that talk of detecting was making me nervous. I thought you might be training to become a PI."

"It's a shame she's not," said Pat. "She'd be a fine one. My best student ever, by far."

"We all know I'm your only student," said Bea, rolling her eyes.

"Have to admit, you've got a knack for it, Bea," said Angela.

"Don't worry, she'll be able to take good advantage of it with her new writing career," Pat said.

Bea grimaced as Pat blabbed how she'd come to the inn to give Bea the training to become the Agatha Christie of Napa Valley. "I've taken to calling her J.B. Fletcher Junior." For a PI, Pat was not much good at keeping secrets.

Angela was, as Bea predicted, alarmed by Pat's revelation. But she held her tongue for a moment. The truth was, if Bea wanted to write mystery stories, who was she to try to stop her? Still, then, the inn, BettyCon, and all things Christmas—what, and who, were they doing it for, if not for Betty's Christmas-crazed fans?

She began to respond slowly, carefully. "Bea, you do realize we have an entire business riding on Betty Snickerdoodle now. I don't want to stand in the way of your creativity, but—"

"Good gravy, you worry too much, girlie!" Bea said with a cackle. "I'm going to write sweet mysteries that Betty's fans will like—at least, I think a lot of them will. No blood, no serial killers, just good, clean, murderous fun! And I'm not going to stop writing Christmas stories, either. In fact, I've just come up with a great idea for one about a beautiful young executive who seems determined to choose the wrong guy, even though the right one is right in front of her. I'm thinking of calling the main character Angela."

Angela rolled her eyes but soon found herself giggling. "I'll always be grateful for that wild imagination of yours, Bea."

"And don't worry. After that, I promise I'll do at least one Christmas story every year, along with a mystery or two."

"You know Betty's fans hope for more than one new story a year."

"That's where the writing workshop comes in. Maybe we'll find the next Betty Snickerdoodle. A new talent we could publish. Or maybe a co-author. You're the business brain—I know you'll figure out how to make it work."

Angela thought about it a minute and realized Bea might be right: Maybe she did worry too much.

"We'll be working on your confidence in the New Year, girlie," said Bea.

"We've already got a long list of things to work on, Bea," Angela said, smiling.

"Good thing there's nothing either of us likes more than a challenge!"

~ The End ~

EPILOGUE

Christmas and New Year's came and went.

Angela and her team bore down on the task of readying the inn for BettyCon, now just weeks away. Aside from finishing the construction and decoration of several new casitas and the last few guest suites, there was an agenda to design, catering to arrange, transportation to set, and marketing to execute. It was exhilarating, but exhausting, too. So when an opportunity came to spend an hour or two away from the inn, Angela decided to take it. But as she sat waiting in the little café, she had to laugh at herself. Instead of just relaxing, she studied the menu, watched the staff's workflow, and wondered if she should sample a few of the baked goods for inspiration.

Truth was, the girl loved her work. She didn't really have an off switch.

Right on time, the tall, handsome man she was waiting for walked through the door. He smiled at her so warmly and sincerely, it was like he'd never smiled at her before. She stood up and gave him a hug.

"You look like a new person," she said. Instead of slick designer duds, he looked relaxed in jeans and a button-down shirt. Even his hair looked different—naturally wavy, no longer styled. Still, he looked as gorgeous as ever. Maybe even more gorgeous than ever.

"Do you miss the fancy clothes?" she said with a laugh.

"Not at all," Foxy said. "The car, though—that I miss." He dropped his key chain on the table. The car key attached bore a mid-level brand, and the key itself looked at least a few years old.

"Back to reality, huh? So what happens to a car like that when you're done with it? I assume the FBI must own it?"

"It's being redeployed. A colleague of mine in Miami is using it for his undercover gig. I'm going to get myself a latte. You set for coffee?"

He came back to the table a few minutes later, two large latte cups in hand.

"Thanks, Foxy," Angela said. "Wait—I should ask—is Foxy even your real name?"

"Believe it or not, it sort of is. But it's not from 'Foxworth.' My name's Drew Faulkner. Girls started calling me Foxy Faulkner in middle school."

"Already attracting attention from the ladies in middle school—I guess you were a junior high Casanova?"

"I peaked early."

"Don't be so sure about that," laughed Angela.

"They say that when you use a fake name, it's better to use something you'd naturally respond so. That's why I use Foxy. I don't love it, but if someone says it, I react without having to think about it."

"I guess I should call you Drew, then."

Drew caught Angela up on the details of the case against Lee, Walter, James, Harry, and Frank.

"Those aren't their real names. The details will all come out once they're charged. I bet it's going to be a big story." He went on to explain how he'd been working the case for over a year, gathering evidence of racketeering and tax evasion.

"They've been swindling millionaires and billionaires for several years now, all over the world. Of course, with Eddie's death, they've added murder to their crooked resumes. They probably didn't plan it—it looks like they just wanted to sideline him, at least at first. But the stakes often rise when you're running a racket like theirs. I'm hoping all of them end up in prison for a long time, but I suspect there will be a deal offered to one or two of them to turn on the others. By the way, I almost forgot to mention—they're family. 'Lee' is married to Harry, who's Walter's brother. James and Frank are her sons. It'll be interesting to see if their blood ends up thicker than water."

"Wow, no kidding? Congratulations on nailing them," Angela said.

"I have to confess, you and Bea and your gang ended up helping, even though at first I thought you'd blown my case. I couldn't believe it when I came into the ballroom and the safe was gone."

"Yeah, well… get to know Bea and you'll realize she's always got another trick up her sleeve."

"Aseem's tracker led local cops right to them. Your discovery about the flour was critical, too. I hope you don't mind—I took the liberty of telling Ming you proved it wasn't his fault. He said he never had any doubt, but I could tell he was relieved—both that he was off the hook, and that you were the one to figure it out."

"You actually should take credit for that. If

Foxy hadn't been in the kitchen where he didn't belong, I doubt I would have looked into those ingredients," Angela said. "By the way, do you have any idea how Walter and James broke into the control room? Aseem said he couldn't figure it out. His video shows them waltzing right in, but it's not clear how."

"That's one of the most interesting bits of the case," Drew said. He explained that the answer stemmed from the night Aseem was attacked. "When Walter and James flipped Aseem over after knocking him out, it was so they could take images of his fingers. Then they used special ink and conductive paper to create a fake fingerprint. Then they used their fake print to fool the scanner on the control room door." He shook his head with disbelief and took a sip of coffee. "It required so much smarts and precision to do it, then they stupidly left some of the paper right by the door. And they left the ink cartridge in the printer in the business center, too. I shouldn't complain about smart criminals making stupid mistakes, though. That's my bread and butter."

As they chatted, Angela found it was easy to talk to Drew—even easier than talking to Foxy. Underneath the fake Foxy facade, Drew was just a straight-up nice guy, with a delightful sense of humor, too.

"So, Angela, thank you for meeting me. Mainly, I wanted to apologize in person for my Foxy routine. I had to make sure I fooled Lee and her gang. And I wanted to get close to you to be sure you weren't in on it. Ditto about the liquor license thing —I would never have outed you to McGregor."

"No need to apologize. I'm glad to have played a role, even an unwitting one, in bringing those crooks down. Besides, Foxy's flirting was over the top, but it was still fun—even though it was fake."

Drew paused and tentatively picked up Angela's hand. "It wasn't all fake. I wasn't lying when I said you were an amazing woman, Angela."

Angela felt another warm blush appearing on her cheeks. But this time, it was nice. Unlike the overwhelming steam that Foxy's charm offensive generated, Drew's sincere sweetness didn't make her feel uncomfortable. On the contrary, it made her feel happy and relaxed.

"I'll be heading out of town for a few weeks, working on another case in Reno," Drew said. "Then I'll be back home to San Francisco for a while. When I do… I was wondering if you might like to go out sometime. Your conference will be behind you by then—we'll both be ready for a little fun, I'd imagine."

"I think I'd like that," Angela said, after a pause that felt just a little too long.

"Oh good," said Drew. "The way you hesitated, I thought maybe you'd gotten together with Aseem. I just… I had the impression there might be history there."

"We do have a history—a long history of being dear friends. Neither one of us plans to change that." Though she thought it, she stopped herself from adding, "at least not at the moment." Because the truth was, she'd come to believe Aseem was right. They were too good together at work to risk screwing it all up.

"Good," said Drew, gently kissing the back of Angela's hand. Then he raised his coffee cup for a toast. "To new beginnings."

"To new beginnings," Angela replied, clinking her coffee cup lightly against his.

FROM THE AUTHOR

Thank you for choosing and reading my book!

If you enjoyed it, I hope you'll consider leaving a rating or review on Amazon, Goodreads or BookBub. Reader reviews help others discover new books they'll enjoy.

I love staying in touch with readers! If you'd like to connect, please sign up for my newsletter at pepperfrostauthor.com

or just email me: pepper@pepperfrostauthor.com.

By signing up for my newsletter, you'll be alerted about new releases. Another way to be among the first to know is to follow me on Bookbub at bookbub.com/authors/pepper-frost.

I'm so grateful for your support!

♥ Pepper

BOOKS BY PEPPER FROST

The Return of Betty Snickerdoodle (A Betty Snickerdoodle Mystery #1)

A Sleuth Is Born (A Betty Snickerdoodle Mystery #2)

Bake It Like Betty (A Betty Snickerdoodle Mystery #3)

Mixed to Death (A Betty Snickerdoodle Mystery #4)

Murder Takes a Bough (A Betty Snickerdoodle Mystery #5)

Of Mice and Murder (A Betty Snickerdoodle Mystery #6)

BOX SET: Betty Snickerdoodle Mysteries (1-3)

BOX SET: Betty Snickerdoodle Mysteries (4-6)

Free for newsletter subscribers (sign up at pepperfrostauthor.com):

Betty's Big Game (a Betty Snickerdoodle short story)

www.ingramcontent.com/pod-product-compliance
Lightning Source LLC
Chambersburg PA
CBHW030353310726
48979CB00001B/288